# Also by P. J. Hoover

**_Tut: My Immortal Life_ Series**
_Tut: The Story of My Immortal Life_
_Tut: My Epic Battle to Save the World_

**_The Forgotten Worlds_ Trilogy**
_The Emerald Tablet_
_The Navel of the World_
_The Necropolis_

# THE CURSE OF HERA

## CAMP HERCULES VOLUME 1

## P. J. HOOVER

ROOTS IN MYTH, AUSTIN, TX

This is a work of fiction. All of the characters, organizations, and events portrayed in this novel are either products of the author's imagination or are used fictitiously.

THE CURSE OF HERA
Camp Hercules Volume 1

A Roots in Myth Book
Austin, TX
For more information, write
pjhoover@pjhoover.com
www.pjhoover.com

ISBN: 978-1-949717-00-6 (trade paperback)
ISBN: 978-1-949717-03-7 (ebook)

First edition: October 2018

FOR MADELINE, FOR TAKING A
CHANCE ON ME

 # CHAPTER 1

I raised the spear and got ready to throw it into the Hydra's heart. Well, at least where the heart would be, if the Hydra were real. Hopefully it would work the same. The fake Hydra would be dead.

"Not the spear!" Daniel shouted just as the thing flew from my hand.

It hit hard, right on the Hydra's chest. Hit and bounced off. I barely had time to jump out of the way before one of the Hydra's heads lashed down at me and tried to make a snack of my arm.

"What is this thing made of?" I yelled over to Daniel. Except with the yellow bandana covering my mouth, it came out a little muffled.

"Use the sword!" Daniel shouted. "Cut off its head!"

Its head. That was some kind of joke since there were

nine heads. Another head darted down and tried to eat me. I rolled out of the way, through the thick red mud. This was the worst summer camp ever.

I grabbed the sword from my waist. Camp Rule Number Four said I had to carry it everywhere, and for once, I didn't disagree with the stupid rules. Not that I was some sword champion. But it couldn't be much different than swinging a baseball bat, could it?

I swung the sword, and the stupid Hydra twisted away, almost like it was doing a fun little dance.

Harper stepped in front of me. "Do you have any idea how to swing a sword?" she asked, and then she shoved me away, raised her sword, and sliced one of the heads off the Hydra.

Blood and guts spewed everywhere, drenching me, Harper, and Daniel. Which was impossible. How could a robotic Hydra monster have such realistic blood and gore?

"Nice shot," I said, wishing I'd spent more time listening when the camp counselors were giving us sword lessons.

I couldn't tell if she blushed since she was covered in blood.

"Not that head!" Daniel shouted.

Harper and I immediately turned to look. From the stump where the head had been, two brand new heads grew.

"Are you kidding me?" I shouted. "That is completely not fair."

The stupid thing now had ten heads, all of which were fixed on us, ready to tear us to shreds.

Daniel looked at me and Harper like we'd forgotten our brains at home. "Don't you guys know anything about the Hydra?"

That brought us back to how this entire mess started.

# CHAPTER 2

Let's just say it all started back in November when I woke up and Mom wasn't there. I knew this because I had to grab my own freezer waffles and pop them in the toaster. This never happened. The only time Mom ever left me alone was when she went to the grocery store because she said I was a pain in her backside and never stopped complaining.

I noticed the note on the kitchen table when I was dumping way too much syrup onto my waffles. It was written on Mom's signature owl stationary.

BE RIGHT BACK! LOVE, MOM.

I dumped a little more syrup on the waffles and sat down to eat right as the door opened.

"You're awake!" she said, rushing in. She dropped her huge, yellow purse onto the table and planted a giant kiss on my head.

"Where were you?" I asked, squirming out from under her kiss.

"Ooooh . . . ," she said. "I was hoping you'd still be asleep, but it took forever."

"What took forever?"

She pressed her lips together and clenched her fist. "I am so horrible at keeping secrets. Do you want to know?"

Horrible at keeping secrets didn't even begin to describe it. Mom would be the worst spy in the universe. If she ever got captured, all they would have to do was look at her funny, and she'd tell them everything.

"What's it about?" I asked, trying to play the game with her, since I knew she wanted to tell me.

Mom reached for her purse. "It's about this summer."

This summer! Mom had to be talking about the football camp at the University of Texas. I was dying to go to this camp. It was crazy hard to get into and way expensive, but everyone said it was the best week in the history of time. You got to practice one on one with the actual college football players, and if you were super lucky and signed up early enough, you had a chance of winning season tickets for the fifty yard line.

"Is it about camp?" I said, trying not to get too excited. But who was I kidding? This was going to be epic.

Mom's eyes got really wide. "How did you know? Did Daniel say something?"

5

"Daniel?" I held my face still. "Daniel doesn't play football." Daniel was this kid that lived down the street, and sure, our moms were like best friends, but Daniel and I never hung out together. As far as I knew, Daniel read books and played *Magic: The Gathering* at the local comic book store all the time.

"Football?" Mom said. "What do you mean football?"

Uh oh. This was not how I imagined the conversation going.

"I thought you were talking about the football camp at UT," I mumbled through a bite of waffle.

Mom's face relaxed and she let out a small laugh. "Oh, no. I didn't sign you up for football camp."

I tried not to let complete and utter disappointment register on my face. But no football camp! That was the worst. Maybe there was still time. It was only November.

"What camp did you sign me up for then?" I asked. It must be one of the sports camps at the high school. Not that they sold out or anything, so why would she need to sign me up this early?

Mom blew out a deep breath and couldn't keep a huge smile from creeping onto her face. "Are you ready for this?"

I nodded.

"Okay, Logan," Mom said. "I knew you were really sad that you couldn't visit your father this summer, and I didn't want you to be bored out of your mind while I was at work every day, so I signed you up for . . . Camp Hercules! I got you in for all six weeks!" She almost jumped out of her seat in excitement.

"Camp . . . Hercules?" I said. It sounded kind of familiar . . . maybe? Except not like something I'd want to do, especially for six weeks. Why did Dad have to shift his plans so I couldn't come visit this summer? This was all his fault.

She grabbed my hand which was covered in syrup. "Oh, Logan, I hope you're so excited. I went with Daniel's mom at midnight and we spent the entire night sleeping outside to save our place in line. Do you know they sold out five people after us? We barely got in. And I've been saving up for this from the moment they first started advertising. Are you happy?"

Her eyes were really wide, and she wasn't even complaining about all the syrup I'd put on my waffles, and even though I had no idea what Camp Hercules was (though I was pretty sure it was not a football camp), I couldn't crush Mom's happiness.

I forced myself to smile the cheeriest smile I could. "Yeah, Mom. I'm really excited."

Mom couldn't take it anymore. She jumped up and hugged me. "Oh, good. I am so relieved. But I'm going to get some sleep, and you need to get to school."

That was how I got signed up for Camp Hercules.

# CHAPTER 3

I tried to ignore all my friends when they started talking about the amazing summer they were going to have . . . at football camp. I really tried. But when we actually got in the car to drive to Camp Hercules, I kind of lost it.

Daniel plopped into the seat next to me. Mom was still at the door, chatting with his mom, probably about all the fun things they were going to do while we were off suffering through some stupid camp for the entire summer.

"I cannot believe it's finally here!" Daniel said. He shoved his glasses up higher, and then he blew his nose, really loud.

"Are you kidding?" I said. "You're excited about this camp?"

Daniel and I were not friends. I was pretty sure we'd said all of ten words to each other this entire school year, half of those consisting of not real words but more head-nods while passing each other in the hallway. That counted. It wasn't that I didn't like Daniel. When we were younger and our moms got together, we hung out all the time. But that was for things like bouncy houses and birthday cake. Baby stuff that everyone had in common.

Daniel fixed his eyes on me so intently, I thought he was going to drill a hole through my head with his stare.

"Logan," he said. "Do you have any idea what people would pay to take your spot for Camp Hercules?"

"You mean I could have sold my ticket?" I said. That would have been awesome! I could have made money and not had to go to this dumb camp.

"Do you even know what Camp Hercules is?" he said.

I shrugged. I'd spent the last six months trying to pretend today wasn't going to come. Like maybe the earth would implode instead. But then Mom had come home with a brand new sleeping bag and canteen and entire box filled with other things she insisted I needed, and I knew there was no getting out of it.

"Not really," I said. Mom got in the car, so I lowered my voice.

"Okay," Daniel said, super serious. "Camp Hercules is a camp where we get to immerse ourselves in the world of mythology, by doing the exact same labors that Hercules did."

I wasn't sure what language Daniel was speaking, but he didn't really clear up my confusion. Mythology? Labors? This was going to be even worse than I thought.

I nodded and Daniel kept talking, and pretty soon we got to camp. There was huge statue of some lady wearing a blindfold and a toga holding a sign like the Statue of Liberty holding her torch.

"I don't get to come in?" Mom said.

"If you're going to miss me, I could always skip it," I said in one last effort to get out of camp.

"Oh no," Mom said, and she unlocked the doors. "I know how excited you are about this. I'll be fine."

I leaned forward and gave her a kiss on the cheek, and then Daniel and I got out with all our stuff.

There was a huge line of kids, probably over a hundred,

standing outside the walls of camp. And these walls . . . well, from way back here, they looked like they were painted shiny gold and tall enough to keep in a T-Rex. There was a massive gate leading into camp, and above it hung a sign with some funny jar thing on it and really weird looking letters.

## ϹΑΜΡ ΗΕΡϹυΛΕϹ

Once I passed through that gate, there would be no turning back.

We hauled our stuff over to the line, standing behind some girl with short blond hair. She whipped around to face us.

"I saw Hercules," she said, shoving something that looked like a pen into her pocket.

Daniel's eyes got really wide. "You did not."

She nodded. "I did. He was standing on the fence like five minutes ago. I can't believe this is really happening. We are going to have the best time."

Because she seemed pretty cool, and because there was no way to get out of it now, I nodded and tried to pretend she was right. That this was going to be a great time.

"I'm Harper," she said.

"I'm Logan, and this is Daniel," I said.

"Nice to meet you guys," Harper said, and then she craned her neck back around and tried to spot Hercules again.

We finally made it up to the giant gate. Three old ladies were there checking us in. All three had spiky gray hair, super dark sunglasses, leather pants, and tank tops, making them look like some sort of geriatric punk rock band. To make the look even more complete, they each had a different streak of color in their gray hair that matched their tank top: red, yellow, and blue. Between the three of them, they had one iPad.

The lady in the middle in the yellow held the iPad out to me. "Hey, Sugar Plum, find your name on the list and check the little box next to it." At least that was what came out of her mouth. But in my mind, her words got all jumbled. Like I swear she told me I was going to stub my toe on a boulder and lose a toenail. It was so random.

"What?" I said.

"Your name, Sweetie," she said again, sounding really annoyed that I'd asked. "Check the box next to it on the screen." She tilted her head down like she was staring right at me, but I couldn't tell since her sunglasses were so dark. I knew I didn't want to see what was under her sunglasses.

I scanned through all the names until I came to mine, then I clicked the little box next to it. It immediately highlighted green. I guess that meant I was officially in. Mom staying up all night to sign me up had really succeeded. Here I was.

"Head on through the gate," the lady to the left with the red streak in her hair said. "Sorting will be at the base of Mount Olympus at ten o'clock."

Mount Olympus. Whatever. This was getting dorkier by the second.

"And watch your step," the lady on the right with the blue streak said.

"Yeah, okay." I headed through the gate to wait for Daniel. Seeing as how he was the only person I knew here, I guessed we'd be hanging out together.

I spotted Harper and hurried over to join her. She was studying a paper map.

"Do you know where Mount Olympus is?" she asked.

I looked over her shoulder at the map, trying to make sense of anything. But everything looked like it was written in a different alphabet.

"No idea," I said. "This place is really big."

"Yeah, my mom told me it used to be some little kid amusement park," Harper said.

"Kiddie Acres," Daniel said, walking up to join us. "Do you remember my five-year-old birthday party, Logan? I had it here."

"You did?" I tried to remember, and slowly little bits and pieces came back to me. "Was there like a tiny little Ferris wheel and a train?"

"Yes!" Daniel said. "And ponies. Remember when you cried on the ponies?"

My face got really hot. I'd always been a little freaked out by ponies but never knew why.

"Didn't Kiddie Acres close down a few years ago?" I asked, trying to change the subject. Maybe it closed down because the pony rides were terrifying.

"It did," Harper said. "That's what my mom told me. She said some private corporation bought it and put up that giant wall, and no one knew what was going on until they started advertising camp. She hired someone to wait in line to sign me up since we live in DC."

"You don't live here?" I just figured that everyone here

was from Texas. But there were a lot of kids.

"People are here from all over the country, Logan," Daniel said. "I told you this was a big deal."

I was saved from having to say anything else because just then a giant drum started beating.

"It's almost ten!" Harper said. "We're going to be late. And I am not getting sorted into some lame labor like that stupid belt." She took off running.

I had no idea what she was talking about, but I figured I was going to find out. I glanced at Daniel, and then we both ran after her. But I wasn't looking where I was going, and I stubbed my toe on a rock.

"Ow!" I said, grabbing my foot.

Suddenly my skin crawled. I was sure I was being watched. I turned back to the gate, and there were the three old ladies, looking my way.

*That one's free,* they seemed to say.

I scowled and looked away. But I did make sure to watch where I was running.

 **CHAPTER 4**

**W**e were the last kids to arrive. All the other kids stood there, holding giant duffel bags and backpacks and sleeping bags. I dropped my stuff to the ground and tried to figure out where we were.

"That is Mount Olympus," Daniel said with awe in his voice.

Okay, I'm going to admit that this part was a little weird. Because here we were at an old kiddie amusement park in Austin, Texas, a city which definitely does not have mountains at all, but ahead of us was what could only be described as a mountain. It was so wide around I had to turn my head to see it all, and it reached way up, so high that the top disappeared into the clouds. A bunch of giant birds flew around, dipping in and out of the clouds. Probably buzzards. We had them all over the place here in Texas. But mountains? We didn't have mountains.

Harper grabbed something from her pocket and held it up. It was the pen thing she'd shoved in her pocket earlier. She pressed something, and it made a little clicking noise. I was about to ask what it was, when the drum beat sped up. The entire group of kids let out a huge gasp.

I turned back to the mountain. Walking down the slope, carrying some kind of yellow and black jar thing, was this guy who had more muscles than anyone I'd ever seen in my life. Like I never knew it was possible to have that many muscles. They bulged and popped with every step he took. He put The Rock to shame. He wore brown pants that were kind of shiny in the sun, almost like they were made of leather. Except who wears leather pants in the summer in Texas? And he wore a golden tank top that sparkled like it had sequins on it. It looked like a costume some pro-wrestler would wear.

"It's Hercules!" Harper said, and she shoved past me, pushing her way to the front.

"Come on," Daniel said, and grabbed my arm, dragging me along.

We were still about four kids deep when Hercules—or whoever the guy pretending to be Hercules was—finally reached the bottom. He took forever, like he was some kind of movie star walking the red carpet.

"You think they hired an actor?" Harper said. Her eyes were so wide, I thought they might fall out of her head.

"They must've," Daniel said. "But I swear that guy looks just like Hercules."

I busted out laughing.

"What?" Daniel said.

"Looks just like Hercules? What does that even mean?"

Daniel narrowed his eyes as if he was trying to figure out my words. "I mean he looks just like Hercules."

"Hercules," I said. "As in some made-up guy from hundreds of years ago. That doesn't make sense."

"First off," Daniel said. "It was thousands of years ago. And second off, he was not made-up. There are statues and paintings and all sorts of historical documents written about him."

"Whatever you say." If Daniel wanted to immerse himself in this silly world of make-believe, that was his choice. I certainly wasn't going to do it.

'Hercules' walked toward a giant golden rock and set the jar thing down on it. The drums beat eight times and then went silent.

"My name is Hercules," he said, flexing his biceps. "I want to welcome you lucky, lucky campers to our first time ever Camp Hercules! This is guaranteed to be your most exciting, adventurous, mythology-filled summer ever!" It didn't look like he had a microphone on, but his voice boomed across the entire base of Mount Olympus. I bet they'd made the whole thing out of paper mache.

Every kid around me started clapping and cheering, and I felt like a complete imposter because it was obvious that everyone wanted to be here except me.

Hercules flexed his triceps and then silenced the crowd. "Camp Rule Number One. Every morning, every camper touches Lucky Rock. No exceptions." He reached down and touched the golden rock. "Failure to follow the rules could be deadly."

"Deadly," I said in a mocking tone. "Please."

Daniel smacked my arm. "You better touch the rock, or I'm not hanging out with you."

I didn't want to lose my only friend before camp even started. That would make for a really long summer.

Hercules cleared his throat and everyone got quiet again. "And now, it's the time you've all been waiting for." He lifted his arm, as if to look at his fingers, but then he actually just flexed his muscles, like he was posing for some body building competition.

"Is this guy kidding?" I said.

"Shhh . . . ," Daniel said. "We're about to get sorted."

"Sorted? What doe—"

"Shhh . . . ," Daniel said again.

A bunch of older kids stepped forward and stood in pairs, guy and girl, to the sides of Hercules. Maybe they weren't even kids. They could have been in their twenties. But they were all super fit which gave me some hope that at least I'd be getting a workout in during camp. Each set had different colored shirts on, and wore the same leather pants as Hercules.

"These are your camp counselors," Hercules said, using the arm he wasn't flexing to motion at them. "Demigods I'm sure you all recognize. Jason, of the Argonauts."

One of the guys stepped forward and nodded.

"Atalanta," Hercules said. "Fierce hunter and warrior."

A girl stepped forward and scowled like she wanted to

fight each of us to the death. Man, I hoped I didn't get put in her bunk.

This whole thing went on and on as each of them got introduced. Achilles. Helen. Theseus. Harmonia (though Daniel kept insisting she was really a goddess). And I had to give this Camp Hercules place credit. They'd really gone all out with this mythology stuff. Each of these 'demigods' had some amazing quest they'd been the hero on, like fighting a Minotaur and stuff like that. If it wasn't totally dorky, it actually would have been really cool.

Okay, it was kind of cool anyway, but I wasn't admitting that to anyone.

"Now, one by one," Hercules said, "Step forward, touch Lucky Rock, and reach into the amphora. Pull out one tile. It will sort you into your labors."

The guy, Jason, stepped up and whispered something in Hercules' ear. Hercules nodded.

"Your bunks, I mean," Hercules said. "But whatever you're sorted into will be the labor that your entire bunk will be responsible for this summer."

I didn't know what any of this labor stuff was, except that it sounded like we were some kind of prison chain gang, picking up trash on the side of the highway. Still, I got in line with Harper and Daniel and waited my turn to get sorted.

I was ahead of Daniel. "So I just reach into the jar and grab something?" I said.

"Amphora," the guy, Jason, said. "But first, touch the rock." He looked like some kind of forest ranger, with a beard and dark hair that reached his shoulders. Kind of like a guy you might expect to scale sheer rock walls for fun.

I leaned down and touched Lucky Rock and was about to reached for the amphora, when this wave washed over me, and all of a sudden, I felt a lot stronger. Or maybe I just had more energy. It was probably the waffles from breakfast finally kicking in.

I reached into the amphora. It was painted yellow and had a bunch of little black pictures all over it, of animals and people and chariots and stuff like that. Inside, I felt a bunch of small plastic tiles. I grabbed one and pulled it out.

"Team Hydra," Jason said. "That's my bunk."

Sweet. Maybe summer wouldn't be so bad. Jason seemed pretty cool.

Daniel was next, followed by Harper. They both got Team Hydra, just like me. At least I'd know people in my bunk.

Once everyone was sorted, Hercules grabbed the amphora and raised it over his head. I think he did it to show off his muscles. "Camp Rule Number Two. No one ever touches the amphora again. Ever. Doing so could have deadly consequences."

Daniel shot me a look, daring me to say something. I shook my head but kept quiet. I didn't want to get on Jason's bad side before we'd even made it back to the bunk.

Hercules tucked the amphora under one of his giant arms. "I'll give you each a piece of advice, learned from my many years of experience with the labors. Never let your guard down. Assume everything can kill you. And whatever you do, never break the camp rules. The Fates will not be kind to you." With those final words of wisdom, Hercules started back up the slope of Mount Olympus, carrying the amphora.

"He sure is serious about these rules," Harper said.

"And all the death threats," I said. "Like our moms would have signed us up for a dangerous camp." Mom freaked out if I rode my bike without a helmet.

"I'm not breaking the rules," Daniel said. "And I suggest you guys don't either."

We grabbed our bags and met up with Jason and the girl named Atalanta.

"You're my favorite demigod, Atalanta," Daniel said. His eyes were huge, like he was stuck in major hero worship, even though she was probably just some college kid working here for the summer.

"Aw, that's so sweet," Atalanta said, and then her eyes darkened. "And just for the record, everyone here calls me Atty, or you will be tasting my fist."

She put up her fist for effect, and every single kid, me included, shrank back, because this Atty girl was seriously fierce. Like her eyes told me she would rip my arms and legs off if I made her mad.

I was not going to make her mad.

# CHAPTER 5

I'd been to summer camp once, back when Mom signed me up for Cub Scouts because she thought I needed more of a male influence since she and Dad were divorced. Anyway, at Cub Scout camp, the cabins were built in maybe nineteen sixty, smelled like old chickens, and had roaches. So that's what I was expecting, except maybe a little newer.

We rounded the corner of a huge clump of trees, and there was a Greek Temple, exactly like the kind on the brochure for camp Mom had pinned to our bulletin board. Like it was made of white stone and had huge columns and a stone patio and everything. On the temple were written the words TEAM HYDRA.

"This is the best camp ever," Daniel said, and he ran up the steps and went inside.

There were twelve of us kids total, six boys and six girls.

Atty and the girls went off to the right, and we followed Jason off to the left. It was two of us to a room, so Daniel and I bunked together.

"Okay, what is all this labor stuff everyone keeps talking about?" I said. I unrolled my sleeping bag and placed it on the mattress and then shoved my bag on a shelf.

"The twelve labors of Hercules," Daniel said, as if that explained everything.

I waited for him to go on.

"You know," he said, like that would help.

"Let's just pretend I forgot," I said. Was this something I was supposed to know? Because if I really was going to be picking up trash or making license plates all summer, Mom was going to have some serious explaining to do.

Daniel started unpacking his bags and shoving stuff into drawers, so I figured I should do the same. I grabbed my bag back off the shelf and opened my dresser.

"So Hercules had to do these twelve really hard things," Daniel said. "In mythology, they're known as his labors."

"Oh." That made a lot more sense. There were twelve different bunks and twelve different labors. "So what kind of things did he have to do?"

Daniel started listing them off on his fingers. "He had to slay the Nemean Lion. He had to kill the Lernaean Hydra. He had to capture the Ceryneian Hind. He had to—"

I put up my hand to stop him, because otherwise, I knew he was going to rattle off all twelve.

"So he had to fight a bunch of these monsters from mythology?" I said.

"Epic, right?" Daniel said. "But he's a demigod, so he got them all done, even when his evil stepmother, Hera, thought he was going to fail. She's the one that made him do the things in the first place. Of course it made her really mad that he got them done. But she was really mean. All the stories say so."

So stepmothers got a bad rap in mythology, just like in fairy tales? Maybe next summer Mom could sign me up for a fairy tale camp. I could get sorted into the Humpty Dumpty bunk. I just hoped that if Dad ever remarried, it wouldn't be to some hag like this Hera person.

I swear I heard a rumble of thunder, but outside the window, the sky was bright blue. There wasn't a cloud in sight. It was probably my imagination.

"But we're not going to be fighting lions here at camp," I said.

Daniel clenched his fists, like he was trying to contain his excitement. "You really don't know what we're going to do?"

I tried to speak very clearly, so I wouldn't have to repeat myself fifty times over the next six weeks. "I don't know anything. Nothing. That's what I know. I don't know about any of this mythology stuff. I don't know what a demigod is. I don't know anything."

He let my words sink in, and then he nodded. "Okay. We got this, Logan. Don't worry."

"I'm not worried," I said. "I just want you to know that I don't know a thing. But I get it. Hercules had these labors. But what are we going to do?"

"We're Team Hydra," Daniel said.

"Uh huh. And . . . ?"

"Well, it's my first time here also," Daniel said. "But I'm pretty sure that means we're going to fight and kill the Hydra."

Fight and kill the Hydra. This was getting better every second.

"And a Hydra is . . . ?"

Jason popped his head into our room. "Lunch and then afternoon activity. We got lucky, guys."

"What did we get?" Daniel asked.

They were either talking about lunch or the afternoon

activity. If it was lunch, I hoped it meant we got pizza.

Jason grinned. "Weapons crafting. We start at one." He threw us each a bright yellow T-shirt and a yellow bandana. The shirt had a picture of some muscly dude that I'm guessing was supposed to be Hercules fighting a monster with a bunch of heads.

I set mine down on the bed.

"Got to put the T-shirts on," Jason said. "Camp Rule Number Three. Wear your T-shirt and bandana at all times."

My T-shirt was going to get pretty smelly if I did that, but I pulled it over my head anyway. It clung to my body like it was tight, but it also moved really easily, almost like a second skin. I twisted around a couple times to test it out. It wasn't like anything I'd ever tried on before.

"Good," Jason said. "If I catch you with your shirt off, I'll shave your head."

That seemed a little severe. I hoped he was kidding. Yet I was pretty sure he wasn't.

# CHAPTER 6

Our bunk and a bunk wearing blue shirts headed to weapons crafting. Turned out our girl camp counselor, Atalanta—oh, I mean Atty—ran it.

"I am a blacksmith," she said once all twenty-four of us sat around in a circle on the ground.

I stifled a laugh.

"Something funny, Logan?" Atty said. She fixed her dark eyes on me so hard, they almost drilled holes through my head. It made me squirm.

I shook my head. "Nothing."

"Good," Atty said. "Because if there's one thing that's not funny about this entire camp, it's the weapons. Your weapons are the only way you're going to stay alive. Which brings me to Camp Rule Number Four: Carry your sword with you at all times."

Daniel's hand shot up. "I don't have a sword," he said before she had a chance to call on him.

"Yeah, I know," Atty said. "That's why you're here. Today we're making swords."

She reached to the ground and grabbed a giant cardboard box, and with her bare hands, she ripped it into long strips. Just watching the muscles in her arms when she did this made me want to lift weights for the next year. Atty tossed us each a long strip of the cardboard. Then she grabbed a box of aluminum foil and handed it to Harper who sat closest to her.

"Everyone take a sheet of aluminum foil and pass it on," Atty said.

This right here was exactly one of the reasons I didn't want to go to some lame camp. Lame camps meant lame craft activities, like making swords out of cardboard and aluminum foil. This was pathetic. But I didn't want to get the death stare again, so when Daniel handed me the box, I grabbed my sheet of foil and passed it on.

I wrapped my cardboard in the foil and tucked in the edges just like she showed us, leaving enough of the cardboard out for the handle of the sword. Atty went from person to person, nitpicking every single little thing. I had to re-do my foil two more times before it was good enough for her.

"Last thing is to spray protectant on it," Atty said. She handed Harper what looked like a can of spray paint, but when Harper sprayed it at her sword, it came out clear.

"Is this for waterproofing?" I said. Since the cardboard handle was still showing, that made the most sense.

Atty fixed those eyes on me again. "Logan, where do you

think you are?"

I shrank down under her gaze. "Camp Hercules?" I said.

"Yeah, Camp Hercules," Atty said. "And what do you think we're going to be doing here? Singing in the rain like Mary Poppins?"

"Um . . ." I had no idea how I was supposed to respond.

"Well, let me tell you," Atty said, and she got right in my face. "You are part of Team Hydra. That means you and the other eleven of your bunkmates—and no one else, so don't think you can count on any of the other bunks—are going to be finding and slaying the Hydra. And for that, you are going to need a sword, not an umbrella. Does that make sense?"

There was no way I was saying no. I nodded and grabbed the clear spray paint can when it came my way. She watched me the whole time, so I made sure to cover all of it before I passed it on.

Atty was crazy. It was going to be a long six weeks.

I don't think I breathed again until she finally dismissed us, telling us we had an hour or so before closing ceremonies for the day.

"Carry our sword everywhere," I said to Harper and Daniel as we walked away. "This camp is ridiculous."

Daniel spun to face me. "Ridiculous? How can you say that?"

"Slay a Hydra?" I said. "For real?"

"Well, yeah, for real," Daniel said. "That was the whole thing about this camp."

"What was the whole thing about this camp?" I said.

"It's supposed to be real mythology," Harper said. "But

I'm going to side with Logan on this one. I don't see how we're going to fight a real Hydra."

Daniel shoved his glasses up on his nose. "Okay, but remember, I warned you guys. When we see that Hydra and I'm the only one prepared, you guys will be sorry you didn't believe me."

I pulled my sword from my scabbard and held it out in front of me. "You're telling me that you actually think we're going to see a real life monster—which is not going to happen, but let's just say it is—and when we do, we're going to use these flimsy little cardboard swords to kill it?"

But Harper and Daniel didn't laugh the way I thought they would. Instead, their eyes were locked on my sword.

"What?" I said.

"Look at your sword," Harper said.

I flipped my wrist around and looked at it. It didn't look flimsy. And it didn't even look like it was made of cardboard and aluminum foil anymore. Instead, it was sleek and smooth and perfectly sharpened. I touched the edge. Big mistake. Blood welled up on my finger.

"I bet it was from the protection stuff," Daniel said, pulling out his sword to look at it.

Both his and Harper's swords looked as realistic as mine. And as sharp. I tucked it back into the scabbard hanging from my belt.

"I'm really impressed with my crafting skills," I said.

Except I wasn't an idiot. This wasn't crafting skills. It was almost like someone had switched out the cardboard swords for these real ones. But I hadn't let the sword out of my sight.

Harper put her sword away and pulled out her map.

"So here we are," she said, pointing at the map. I was willing to trust her. Maps weren't my specialty. "And this is the boundary wall." She drew her finger around the map, where a gold line ran in a sloppy circle.

"That's Mount Olympus," I said, pointing to where we'd been earlier. Not that I was trying to impress her.

Okay, maybe I was, just a little.

"They have a store?" Daniel said, peering over my shoulder. He pressed his finger onto the map to a spot that said TRADING POST. "Do you guys mind if we stop in real quick? I forgot my toothbrush."

Mom had insisted on packing me three toothbrushes, just in case, she said. I wasn't sure how I'd go through three toothbrushes in six weeks, but it was good to know that if I did, I'd be able to buy a new one.

"You can borrow one of mine," I said.

Daniel looked like I'd suggested we share the same toilet paper. "No. I want to get my own."

"Whatever." It wasn't like I had anything else to do.

But Harper stepped back. "I'll catch up with you guys later."

I tried really hard to come up with some reason why we should all stick together, but my mind went blank.

"Sounds good," Daniel said, and he and I set off in the direction of the Trading Post.

It was all the way around Mount Olympus, which meant it took us twenty minutes to get there. A couple kids wearing purple shirts were just leaving. Running out was more like it, as if a monster from mythology had been inside, trying to eat them.

"Wonder what scared them," I said. For a second, I wanted to turn back and forget about shopping for Daniel's toothbrush. But that was ridiculous. This was summer camp. Not scary camp.

Man, my jokes were becoming as lame as this camp.

There were no other campers inside when we walked in. There was actually no one around. But what there was, all over the place, were some epic looking weapons and armor shirts and shields and all sorts of cool stuff.

I grabbed a shield off a shelf and held it in front of me.

"Beware!" I said. "Brave warrior Logan is here to save the day!"

This had to be the dorkiest thing I'd ever said in my life. But the shield had like some magical power that made me feel like a warrior. Made me think I could hunt down any monster, not just the Hydra, and slay it with my mere presence.

"No way!" Daniel said. He grabbed a helmet and put it on his head. Then he straightened his back and put his hands on his hips. "Daniel the hero has come to slay the Minotaur. Beware."

"Dude, you look awesome," I said. "I wonder how much this stuff costs."

"Four years, Sugar Plum," a voice said.

I whipped around to face the counter. Two seconds ago, there had been no one there. But now, the three old ladies with the spiky gray hair and sunglasses stood behind the counter.

"Four years?" I said. "What does that mean?" Maybe it meant four years of hard labor. Six weeks was going to be bad enough.

"Four years off your life, Sweet cakes," the lady in the middle with the yellow streak in her hair said. "Do you want to buy it?" She pulled a ball of green yarn out from under the counter and held it up with one hand. The lady to her right grabbed some scissors as long as my arm and opened them, like she was going to cut the yarn.

"You can't get it back," the old lady on the left said. She held out the iPad. "Just touch the eyeball on the screen if you want to make the deal."

I set the shield back on the shelf. I was pretty sure they were crazy, or else just really great at acting like creepy old ladies, but I also didn't want to find out what they were talking about.

"No, that's okay," I said, though I still kind of wanted the shield.

"That's what I thought," the lady in the middle said. At least that's what she said aloud. But her words got all twisted around again, and in my mind, it sounded more like she said, "You'll be wishing you had that shield pretty soon."

"How about you, Honey bun?" the lady in the middle asked Daniel. "It's five years for the helmet."

Daniel took the helmet off his head and studied it. "It is pretty nice."

"Do you want to buy it?" the lady on the left said.

They did the same yarn and scissor thing, but this time with a ball of blue yarn.

"Ye—" he started, but I was across the room so fast, I could have won sprints at a track meet.

"He doesn't want to buy it," I said, grabbing the helmet from him and setting it back on the shelf.

Daniel almost looked like he was going to get mad, but then he shook his head and said, "Yeah, I don't want to buy it."

Except it was like me with the shield. He did look like he wanted to buy it.

She still held the yarn. "How about the toothbrush? You know you need one, Dumpling."

How did this old lady know Daniel needed a toothbrush? Unless they'd been spying on us.

"How much is it?" Daniel asked.

**34**

The lady on the right with the giant scissors shrugged. "Five minutes. You want it?"

This was the weirdest store I'd ever been into in my life.

Daniel didn't seem nearly as freaked out as I was. He walked to the counter. "What colors do you have?"

The lady on the left got out six different colors and set them on the counter. Daniel picked a yellow one.

"You'll never get another cavity," she said, and held out the iPad for him.

He touched the eyeball on the screen, which lit up green. The lady in the middle measured out a small amount of the blue yarn, and the lady on the right snipped it.

"Let's go." I nearly dragged Daniel from the store.

"Did you hear what they said? I'm never getting another cavity."

"I wouldn't stop brushing if I were you," I said.

We just made it back to the bunk in time. Harper still wasn't back from wherever she'd snuck off to, so the eleven of us, along with Jason and Atty, went to closing ceremonies.

Hercules was just descending from Mount Olympus, flexing his muscles with every step he took. He didn't have the amphora jar thing with him, which meant he was able to flex both arms equally.

"Lower the flag!" he shouted when he reached the bottom.

A guy and a girl counselor whose names I didn't remember stepped forward and took the flag down, folding it up into a triangle.

"Now let me see," Hercules said, scanning the crowd.

"Which bunk gets to protect the flag tonight?"

Just then, Harper ran up, out of breath.

"You guys will not believe what I saw."

I was about to tell her about the trading post, because nothing could have been crazier than that, but Daniel said, "What?"

"The Hydra," she said. "I saw the Hydra."

# CHAPTER 7

Harper had to be joking. But her eyes were huge and she had a grip on my arm so tight I thought she'd puncture my skin. I didn't want to be a jerk, so I decided to play along.

"The Hydra," I said. "Really?"

"Really!" she said. "It was way off, near the boundary fence. I swear."

"How many heads did it have?" Daniel asked.

He couldn't seriously believe her, could he?

Harper shrugged. "I don't know. Ten? Twenty?"

"Was it paper mache?" I asked.

She looked at me like I was crazy. "Paper mache?"

"Yeah," I said. "It can't be real."

I was about to say something else when our counselor Jason smacked my shoulder. "Quiet, Logan," he said. "Hercules doesn't like when people talk at the same time as him."

I turned, and Hercules was staring right at us.

"As I was saying," Hercules said. "The bunk that shall have the flag tonight is . . ." His finger moved across the crowd of kids. Each time it rested on one of the bunks, all twelve kids and both counselors started cheering, like they wanted the stupid flag. Needless to say, when it moved across Team Hydra, I didn't cheer. But Daniel cheered loud enough for all of us.

It wasn't enough. Hercules kept moving, until finally his finger pointed to the last bunk.

"Team Cerberus!" Hercules shouted. "You've worked the hardest today. And your enthusiasm will be rewarded." He walked forward and handed the flag to the camp counselors.

"Stupid Achilles always gets it," Jason muttered. "Like anyone didn't know that was going to happen."

Atty patted him on the arm. "We'll get it tomorrow. Don't worry."

"Why do we want it?" I asked, maybe too loud because Jason whipped around.

"We want it because it represents victory," Jason said.

"Yeah? So what? It's just a flag."

Atty fixed her dark laser eyes on me. It was exactly the same as before. I couldn't look away. "Listen, Logan, it's not just a flag. Don't ever say that again."

I nodded and swallowed. She kept staring at me.

"Whoever gets the flag, gets a day of protection," Atty said. "And protection helps you win the labors. And we want to win our labor, right?"

Our whole team cheered.

"Logan?" she said. "Do you want to win?"

What I wanted was for her to look away.

"Yeah, I want to win," I said, trying to sound all upbeat and into this whole camp thing. "So maybe tomorrow we'll get it."

"We better," Atty said. "Or else everyone in the bunk does ten laps." She finally looked away.

I was pretty sure she didn't mean laps around Lucky Rock, but I didn't dare ask her to clarify, or else she'd probably make me run right now.

We headed toward the dining hall, but Daniel, Harper, and I fell to the back.

"I'm telling you it was real," Harper said.

A real Hydra. This camp was getting crazier every day.

"It was probably a piñata," I said. "And for fun one day, they'll let us find it and smash it, and there will be tons of candy inside."

Harper dug something out of her pocket. It was the pen-sized thing I'd seen earlier when we met her. "Does this look like a piñata?" She held the thing up for us to see.

It had a tiny little screen, like it was part of a super-small camera. On the screen, it looked like it could have been some kind of monster, but it was way too small to tell.

"I can't see anything on that," I said.

Harper shoved the pen camera back into her pocket. "It was moving. It was real."

"Okay, fine, it's probably a robot," I said. "Right, Daniel?"

"They did say we'd be fighting real monsters in the camp brochure," Daniel said. "That was one of the reasons I begged my mom to sign me up."

Real monsters. Daniel begging his mom was the reason I was here also, since our moms were best friends.

"Show me the Hydra in person, or it's not real." I crossed my arms.

"Haters gonna say it's fake," Harper said.

I didn't say a word.

Harper rolled her eyes. "Fine. Later tonight, we sneak out. I'll show you guys."

 **CHAPTER 8**

We tried to sneak out after dinner, but since it was the first night at our bunk, Jason and Atty had like fifty activities planned. And since there were only twelve of us, they would have completely noticed if we'd been gone.

First, we had story time. I tried to not have a good time, but Jason started telling this story about going on an amazing voyage across the sea, fighting all sorts of impossible things, including some crazy bird ladies he called Harpies.

"Harpies like shiny things," Jason said.

"Like magpies!" Daniel said.

"Are magpies shiny?" I said.

"No. Magpies are birds that like shiny things," Daniel said. "Maybe the Harpies were part magpie."

"Could be," Jason said. "Because it sure worked. All we

had to do was lure them away with some gold coins, and the Harpies were history."

"So then you got the fleece?" Daniel said.

I'd followed along enough to know that the fleece was the skin of some lamb. Except the skin was golden, or maybe it was just the fur. Something about it was golden. And the story was epic.

"Do you still have it?" Daniel asked after Jason finished talking.

Man, he was so embarrassing. It was just a story. But Jason stood up and went into his room and came back wearing the golden hair thing. It looked like some giant fur coat that people used to wear in the old days, except there were no arms or anything. He just had it slung over his shoulders.

Daniel reached forward. "Can I touch it?"

I kind of wanted to touch it also, not gonna lie.

"No one touches the fleece," Jason said. "I catch you touching the fleece, I chop a finger off."

Daniel shrank back and closed his fingers into a fist to hide them.

"Unless you're dying," Jason said. "Then it's okay to ask if you can touch it."

It made no sense, because if someone really was dying, they might not be able to ask, but I decided not to point this flaw in his logic out.

"What about you, Atty?" a girl in our bunk asked. I think her name was Kaeley, but I was still getting to know everyone. "Do you have a story?"

Atty took a bite of the apple she was holding. Juice

dripped down her chin, and she wiped her mouth with the back of her hand. "Yeah, I have a story. I have lots of stories." And she launched into some heroic story about fighting a giant pig.

"So this pig," I said. "It was how big?"

I knew the second the words left my mouth, I should have kept quiet. She fixed her eyes on me again. I was pretty sure by this point that Atty hated me.

"It was boar," Atty said. "Not some pig. What do you think? I was fighting Porky Pig? Or Babe? What do you think this is, some cartoon?"

"Um . . . ," I said, because Atty scared me to death.

"So how'd you finally defeat it?" Harper asked.

Atty traced one of her fingernails across her arm, hard enough that blood popped up. "All I had to do was draw blood. Just a little bit. That was enough to slow it down." She took another bite of the apple and tossed the core over her head.

I watched it fly through the air. It hit the ground, and I swear it became whole again. But not just whole. It also turned gold. I blinked, and there it still was, a golden apple sitting on the floor. I started standing, because right now, the only think that mattered to me was picking up that golden apple.

"Sit down, Logan," Atty said.

I sat down.

"Look at me, Logan," she said.

I tore my eyes away from the apple. But then I had to look back.

It was gone. I opened my mouth, though I wasn't sure what I was going to say. Something along the lines of how impossible this whole situation was. But then Jason said, "Time for s'mores!"

Everyone cheered. Everyone except me. I couldn't get that stupid apple out of my head. But then Jason pulled out the marshmallows, and Daniel popped one on the end of a stick. I ate five. After that, my eyes got really heavy, and there was no way I was going to see a Hydra, real or fake.

The next day, we went through the whole routine again, touching Lucky Rock, admiring the amphora. Achilles' bunk raised the flag, and Jason scowled the entire time.

"We'll get it today," Atty said. "We just need to train harder." She glared at me during this last part, like I was the slacker in the group.

During weapons crafting, we made a spear out of our marshmallow sticks and some duct tape. Atty made me re-do mine five times, until she finally said, "Just hope you don't have to use it." So much for positive encouragement.

The first chance we got, after the afternoon activity, Harper dragged us away.

"We're going to see it now," she said, and she led us down a path and through the woods. And speaking of woods, the trees here had to be the tallest trees in Austin, Texas. That wasn't saying much because trees in Austin didn't grow very tall, but these reached way up, like a forest.

"Have you guys noticed the trees?" I said. It was super quiet, except for some birds chirping, so my voice echoed around the entire forest. At the sound of my voice, every-thing went silent. The birds. The crickets. The breeze blowing through the leaves.

We stopped walking, and my hand went immediately to my spear. I gripped it in my fist, but it was really thick, not like the marshmallow stick from earlier. Instead, the same thing happened that had happened with my sword. I wasn't hold-ing some lame marshmallow stick spear with duct tape for a point. I was holding a full-on, seven foot long, spear with a wooden shaft and a metal point that looked like it could pierce one of these trees.

"Um . . . ," Daniel said.

I guess he'd noticed the same thing as me.

"Shhh . . . ," Harper barely said, holding her finger to her lips. She grabbed her sword and held it up, but instead of looking completely awkward like Daniel did, it was like the sword was made for her. She tossed it to her other hand and raised it.

We stood there, and the seconds ticked by. Goosebumps raised on my skin. Something was going to happen.

But nothing did.

"Is this where you saw the Hydra?" I whispered.

She shook her head. "It was closer to the fence."

"Maybe we should head back," Daniel said. For once, instead of looking all excited about this mythology re-enactment camp, he looked like he was about to pee his pants.

"I have to show you guys," Harper said, and she took another step.

A twig snapped under her foot.

There was a huge whooshing sound, like all the air was being sucked out of the forest. Something heavy landed on the ground, out of sight, but ahead of us. The trees bent from the impact. And then the thing started toward us, knocking trees over as it came.

"Run!" Harper shouted.

Run? I needed to see what this thing was, because whatever it was, it's not like it was real or would hurt us. But Harper grabbed my arm and dragged me, and we sprinted back for the tree line. We were almost there when I finally turned around.

A giant boar was tearing through the trees, running right for us.

 **CHAPTER 9**

"We're gonna die!" Daniel shouted.

I sum up Daniel's athletic abilities like this: I was pretty sure he sat out of gym class more than he went, and on the days he went, he wasn't winning any races, even in the slow heat. But his legs started moving at an unbelievable speed. He left me and Harper in the dust and busted through the tree line. Then he kept on running until he was a good fifty yards away.

Harper and I ran to catch up with him. We fell to the ground beside him and turned back to look. If this was the same kind of thing Atty was talking about in her story, she needed to improve her story telling skills, because they came nowhere near to the truth. This thing was huge, probably taller than my house, and it had curved tusks that looked like they could double as airplane wings.

**47**

The giant boar stood there, in the trees, snorting at us and digging its hooves into the earth, making huge chunks of dirt fly through the air.

"The boar!" Daniel said, while he tried to catch his breath. "It's going to kill us."

I set my spear on the ground. "Don't worry. It's not real." Sure, it was scarier than the haunted house Mom had let me go to on Halloween, but it wasn't any different. They were both fake.

"Not real?" Harper said. "Do you see that thing?"

It was still pawing at the ground, but it didn't seem to be able to come any closer to us. There must be some sort of electricity it ran on that kept it inside the trees.

"It's a robot," I said. "Like those robots they have at Disney World. What are they called? Animatronics?"

"That is not a robot, Logan," Daniel said, pointing his spear at the robot boar.

"If it's not a robot, then what is it?" I said. "Tell me that."

"It's a giant boar," Harper said. "Just like in Atty's story."

"Her made-up story," I said.

But Daniel shook his head and put up his hand. "You guys don't know anything about mythology. That is the Erymanthian Boar, the fourth of Hercules' twelve labors."

Twelve labors! This camp . . .

Harper's eyes got wide. "He had to kill that thing?"

"No," Daniel said. "He had to capture it."

Capture it? That was probably worse.

I stood up and grabbed my spear. "A boar is a boar. And remember what Atty said in her story? We need to draw blood. Then it'll go away."

Daniel scooted back even more. "I'm not going near that thing."

I rolled my eyes. "It's not real." I started for the boar, saying this over and over in my mind, because even though there was no possible way it was real, it sure looked real. And sounded real. And each step I took, I got less sure about the fact that it wasn't real.

"That's stupid," I said aloud, even though Daniel and Harper were now out of hearing distance. I was almost to the tree line. I reached out, with the spear, trying to get close enough to scrape it. But the boar grabbed the spear in its mouth, yanked it out of my grip, and tossed it aside. Then it turned back to me and snorted so loudly, my eardrums ached.

"No!" I said. That spear was my best chance, because no way was I getting close enough to use my sword. I shuffled forward, one more step, but tripped over a rock. I landed flat on the ground, only a foot away from the snarling nostrils of the boar. Hot breath tickled the back of my neck. This was the worst situation possible.

Draw blood. That's what I had to do.

My fingers wrapped around the rock, and I sat up and threw the rock as hard as I could at the boar's head.

It wasn't hard enough. And it only made the boar angrier. I scrambled around, looking for another rock, but the most beautiful sight in the world appeared. The spot on its forehead swelled up, into a lump, and a tiny drop of blood popped to the surface, breaking through the skin.

The boar noticed it at the same time as me. It stumbled back. One step. Then two. Then it turned and ran back into the forest, leaving the ground all torn up like someone had started digging a grave. Thankfully not mine.

I grabbed my spear and ran back to Harper and Daniel.

"You did it!" Harper said, and gave me a huge high five.

That was too close.

"Yeah, I did it," I said, and slung my spear over my shoulder. When I was wearing it, it didn't feel as long as it was, like it somehow shrank down.

"I told you guys the Hydra was real," Harper said. "I bet you all the things are real."

"Real fake," I said. "This thing doesn't prove anything." It felt more and more like I was trying to convince myself.

"I think it does," Harper said. "And I have a plan to prove it."

"What plan?" I asked. So far her plan had almost gotten us gored by a robotic monster. But if there really was a way to prove whether all this stuff was real or not, then I was in.

"Tonight after lights out," she said. "Meet me outside the bunk."

 **CHAPTER 10**

I waited until I heard Jason snoring in his room. Then I shook Daniel awake.

"You ready?" I whispered.

He nodded, and we crept out of the bunk, not making a sound. Harper was already out there waiting. She had her blond hair tucked under a black hat, to hide it, but our bright yellow shirts stood out like street signs.

"Maybe we should have changed," I said, pulling at the fabric of my shirt. It was really weird, and I never would have told any of the guys back at school, but even though I'd sweat like crazy during our sword fighting practice earlier today, the shirt didn't smell at all. I'd tried to put on a clean shirt, but Jason had stopped me before I got an arm out.

"What's Camp Rule Number Three?" he'd said, hovering over me like he would glue the shirt on me if I dared to take it off.

I'd let go of the shirt. "What about laundry?"

He'd shaken his head. "Not the shirt," he'd said. "The shirt doesn't get washed."

So I hadn't washed it. And even though it didn't smell, bright yellow wasn't the best color to go sneaking around in after dark.

"Just be stealthy," Harper said, like she was the master of stealth.

She led the way, ducking behind trees and temples and training dummies. We had one close call. We rounded a corner, and there were four of the counselors sitting around a fire pit. I recognized Achilles and his co-counselor Helen (since she was the most beautiful girl I'd ever seen in my life), but I couldn't tell who the other two were since their backs were to us. Maybe Theseus? Or that Harmonia girl?

Harper put a finger to her lips and shook her head. None of us made a sound. I'm pretty sure I didn't breathe. We crept around them, making a huge out-of-the-way circle. Achilles glanced up one time, like maybe he heard my heart beating, but then he looked back at the fire. We continued on, until we finally came to a stop at the foot of Mount Olympus.

"Why are we here?" I said. It looked a lot different with no one else around. There was just a flagpole with no flag (Theseus and his bunk had gotten it this time) and Lucky Rock.

Harper looked at me like I'd missed seeing a movie that everyone else had seen. "We're climbing Mount Olympus."

I looked up at the mountain. "We are?"

"Yeah," she said. "We're going to spy on Hercules. It's the best place to get more information about this camp."

I was sure there was more she wasn't telling me, but she just smiled and waited.

Every part of me knew this wasn't a good idea. I wasn't an idiot. But also, she had a point. If somehow any of this stuff was real, then Hercules would know.

"Great," I said. "Let's go."

Daniel did not agree. "We can't climb Mount Olympus," he said.

"Why?" Harper said. "You scared of heights?"

"Well, yeah," Daniel said. "But that's not it."

"Then what?"

He took a step back. "Because only the gods are allowed on Mount Olympus."

I busted out laughing. "The gods. Okay."

"I'm serious, Logan," he said. "If we climb Mount Olympus and the gods find out, they're going to send us to Tartarus."

"Tartarus?" I said. "What's that?"

"It's a really bad place in the Underworld," he said.

"The Underworld?"

"Do you know anything about mythology?" Daniel said.

"No, I told you that," I said. "I didn't sign up to come to this camp."

"Look," Harper said. "Can we just go already? Someone's going to hear you guys arguing." She started up the side of the mountain.

"I'm not going," Daniel said.

"Okay, stay here." I started after Harper.

Daniel stood there for another ten seconds. Then he reached down, touched Lucky Rock, and started after us.

For being a fake mountain built in the middle of Austin, Texas, Mount Olympus felt completely real. Like gravel slipped under our feet, and dirt got under my fingernails. And the higher we climbed, the cooler the air got.

Daniel slipped a good five times, and each time I worried he was going to topple all the way to the bottom, because it got steeper with each step we took. Also, he was breathing really hard, like he was about to collapse. If there were gods on Mount Olympus, they probably heard it.

"You okay?" I asked for about the fiftieth time.

He nodded. "Fine. Just keep going."

So we did, until finally the ground leveled out.

"We're not at the top yet," I said.

"Quiet!" Harper pointed forward.

There, set into the side of the mountain, was a white temple, sort of like our bunk temples, but way fancier with all sorts of carvings and colored paint and stuff. Out front, with a fountain surrounding it, the amphora sat on a pedestal. It glowed in the darkness of the night. Glowed enough to see that it was being guarded by some kind of unnatural monster. It looked like a bird, with feathers and wings and huge claws, except it had the face of a woman instead of a beak.

"It's a harpy!" Daniel said. "We'll never be able to get past it."

At the sound of his voice, the harpy looked our way. Then it leapt off its perch and flew right at us.

 **CHAPTER 11**

"**D**rop, and don't move!" Harper said. She fell to the ground, flat on her stomach.

Daniel and I did the same. The air whooshed above me, like the harpy had flown over and barely missed me. The second it was gone, we jumped up and ran, toward the wall of the temple. We ducked behind a column just as the harpy flew at us again. And again. Each time we moved around the column. Its claws barely missed us. And it kept shrieking, over and over, piercing through the dark night.

Jason's story came back to me.

"Who has something shiny?" I said, ducking and hiding so I didn't get sliced up like Swiss cheese at the deli.

"Shiny?" Daniel said.

"Yeah. Jason said harpies like shiny things."

Understanding dawned on his face. Except then he

reached for his pocket and shook his head.

"She can't have it," Daniel said.

The harpy shrieked and dove at us again. Not only was she ready to kill us, she smelled horrible, like she slept in sewers and ate bad oysters.

"This is not the time to be sentimental," Harper said. "If you have something shiny, we need it now."

Maybe the harpy liked shiny things so much that she could smell them, because she seemed to focus in on Daniel, and started attacking only him. She sliced at his shoulder, hard enough that he let out a cry before pulling his arm away. Then he reached into his pocket and pulled out a coin.

"It's my lucky quarter," Daniel said. He started to wrap his fingers around it, so I grabbed it and threw it before he got a chance.

The harpy was after it in a second, darting off into the darkness of the night, vanishing over the side of Mount Olympus, leaving us behind.

"Are you hurt?" Harper said, pulling up the sleeve of his shirt.

This could be bad. The harpy had really torn at his arm. But not only was the shirt not torn, Daniel's shoulder wasn't even red.

"That's impossible," I said, leaning forward to get a closer look.

"The shirt protected me," Daniel said. "It must be like some kind of armor. Maybe that's why we have to always keep them on."

It made sense and completely didn't make sense all at the

same time. Just like everything about this camp.

"Come on," Harper said. She tiptoed forward, toward a window on the side of the temple.

"Hercules must live here, halfway up the mountain, since he's not a full god," Daniel said. "Maybe only the real Olympian gods live way up there."

"Yeah, the real gods live at the top of this mountain," I said, laughing. But Daniel didn't laugh, and neither did Harper. I caught up to them and soon was looking into the window of the temple.

"He's in there," Harper whispered.

Sure enough, there was Hercules. He stood near a mirror, and I'm not kidding. He was posing, flexing his muscles, looking at his reflection. The window didn't have any glass, so we could hear him talking to himself.

"Happy," Hercules said, and then he placed a huge smile on his face, like he'd won the lottery. "Sympathetic," he said, then his face shifted so it looked like he was in the middle of listening to someone tell a story about their sick grandma. "Smoldering." His face shifted again, this time making it look like he should be on the cover of some outdoor magazine, looking out across the Grand Canyon.

Harper looked at me. She mouthed *OMG* and rolled her eyes.

But Daniel wasn't watching Hercules. Instead, he elbowed me and pointed back to the amphora in the center of the fountain.

It was glowing, even brighter than before, and the pictures on it were moving.

Yes, I realize this is impossible, but the thing was painted yellow and it had black pictures of people, and the people were moving. Like one of them was throwing a spear. And two of them were fighting. Really fighting! Like throwing fists at each other, and some other person was riding a chariot. And the entire thing was completely impossible.

We left Hercules to his facial expressions practice, and walked to the edge of the fountain. Harper pulled the camera pen thing from her pocket and started taking all sorts of pictures.

There was a shrieking cry from behind us. The harpy was coming back. It must've found Daniel's lucky quarter. Before I knew what she was doing, Harper jumped over the rim of the fountain, grabbed the amphora, and then vaulted back over.

"What are you doing?" Daniel said. "You can't do that. That's stealing. Don't you remember Camp Rule Number Two? No one touches the amphora."

She whipped around to face him. "And why do you think that is?"

Daniel held his ground, staring her down. "I don't know."

"Well, I do," Harper said. "It's because there's something going on with this amphora. And we need to get a closer look at it." She grabbed her duffel bag and shoved the amphora inside.

"But Hercules—" Daniel started.

"Will never find out who took it," Harper said. "We'll keep it for a day so I can figure out how it works and get a closer look, and then we'll make sure someone finds it. Someone else besides us."

It was a good plan, if you could get past the part about us stealing it.

The harpy shrieked again. It sounded way closer this time, like it would come over the side of the mountain any second.

"We need to go," I barely whispered.

Daniel looked like he wanted to argue about it some

more, but there was no time. We ducked over the side of the mountain, away from the shriek of the harpy, and scurried down the side as fast as we could move, shoving gravel every which way. We had to get away from here as fast as possible, because it wouldn't take long for the harpy to notice the amphora was missing.

Thirty seconds later, from back up on the mountain, the harpy began to shriek. Overhead, two more harpies flew toward the mountain, maybe to help it search.

"Run!" I said the second we reached the bottom of Mount Olympus. Lucky Rock was just ahead.

But then a voice said, "Where are you three going in such a hurry?"

My stomach hardened into a tight ball of dread. We all three turned to look. There was the camp counselor Achilles, walking right for us. We were caught.

 **CHAPTER 12**

A chilles stabbed his sword into the ground and stood next to it. Unlike the three of us, in our glowing yellow camp T-shirts, he wore a blue camp T-shirt with some picture of a dog that had three heads on it.

"Nowhere," Harper said, slinging the duffel bag over her shoulder.

"Nowhere?" Achilles said. "Camp Rule Number Six: Don't break curfew. If you're going nowhere, then why are you three out after curfew?"

My mind scrambled to think of something. Why did kids sneak out?

"We were hungry!" I said. It was the best excuse in the world. I was always hungry. Except right now. Now I just wanted to get back to the bunk, fall asleep, and wake up, pretending everything impossible that I'd seen was just a dream.

Harpies and pictures moving on the jar thing and a giant boar?

Achilles narrowed his eyes, and I swear he was looking right at Harper's duffel bag. "The dining hall is the other way."

"Oh," I said, because I hadn't thought that far ahead. But whatever. Hunger was a great excuse for anything. "We were going to see if the Trading Post was open."

Achilles took three giants steps toward us and got right in our faces. Daniel tried to shrink back, but Achilles grabbed his shoulders and pulled him close.

"The Trading Post isn't safe after curfew," he said. "Don't ever stay out past curfew. Ever."

Daniel nodded.

"Bad things happen to kids who stay out past curfew," Achilles said. "And if we lose campers our first year, it's going to be really messy. The news alone could shut us down."

At the word 'news,' Harper straightened up and stepped forward. "What's going on at this camp anyway?" she said. "Like who owns this place? And where did you get all the creatures? And what about the mountain? How did you build that?"

Achilles opened his mouth like he was about to answer, but then his cell phone started ringing, playing some heavy metal music that was probably popular thirty years ago. He paused, then pulled the phone from his pocket and put it to his ear.

"Speak to me," he said. Then he listened. Daniel squirmed out of his grip, stepping back. Achilles nodded his head a few times and grunted and said, "I'll be right there." He hung up and stuffed his phone back in his pocket.

"I have to go," he said. "But if I catch you three breaking any of the camp rules again, you get two hours in Tartarus."

That was the scary Underworld place, so I knew he was joking. Except his face didn't look like it was joking, so I didn't say a word. Then he yanked his sword from the ground and ran off, toward the bunks.

"Let's go," Harper said, and we ran back to the bunks, not stopping a single time.

"What are you gonna do with that?" I asked when we got there, nodding at the duffel bag. It wasn't like she could get a better look at it with Jason and Atty hovering over her shoulder.

Harper seemed to realize this at the same time as me. "I'll hide it in the woods."

Daniel shook his head. "I'm not going in the woods."

Boar or not, I couldn't let Harper go into the woods alone at night.

"That's fine," I said. "You go back inside. I'll go with Harper."

Daniel didn't protest in the least. He was inside the bunk and out of sight before we'd even gotten ten feet away.

"As long as we don't make any noise, we should be okay," I said, but I did stay close to Harper. I also kept one hand on my sword, just in case the giant boar came back and tried to kill us.

"Where should we hide it?" Harper asked. It was really hard to see anything in the dark, and once we passed through the trees, it got worse. The trees pressed in at us from all sides.

An owl hooted, breaking the silence of the night, and it startled me so much that I fell forward, against a tree. But my hands went right into the tree, or at least through a hole in the tree.

"I think it's hollow," I said. "Stick the bag in here."

The owl hooted again. Harper stuffed the duffel bag into the hollow opening of the tree, and we hurried back to the bunk. But just as we were leaving the woods, the owl hooted one final time, and I was sure someone was watching us.

 **CHAPTER 13**

Jason woke us early. Way too early, especially since we'd gotten a lot less sleep because of sneaking out past curfew.

"Today we hunt the Hydra," Jason said. He clipped his sword and spear on and pulled his brown hair back into a ponytail.

Hunt that Hydra! Fake or not, that was bound to be epic.

"What about breakfast?" this guy in our bunk named Simon said.

Jason threw us each a granola bar. "There's your breakfast. Now come on. We want to win."

We met up with Atty and the six girls in our bunk outside. Jason and Atty inspected each of us, making sure we had our T-shirts, our bandanas, and our weapons.

"Why the bandana?" Daniel asked. He had it looped

around his wrist, but Jason insisted he tie it cowboy style around his neck.

"Because the Hydra gives off poisonous fumes," Atty said. "That's why. So if you happen to be the one to find the Hydra, put it over your mouth and nose. Otherwise, blood will start coming out of your eyes."

That was a horrible visual. I double checked to make sure my bandana was firmly in place.

"To win," Jason said, "we need to kill the Hydra and bring back the head before any of the other bunks finish their labors."

"Which head?" the kid, Simon, said.

"The head," Jason said. "If you don't know which one, then we aren't going to win. And the other thing is that we stick together. That's the only way we can bring the Hydra down."

We set off, into the forest. I looked around for the hollow tree where we'd stashed the amphora, but in the daylight, everything looked different. And none of the trees looked hollow.

I held my spear in front of me, just in case something jumped out to attack. Images of the boar chasing us filled my mind. Fake or real, I wanted to be prepared if we saw it. We spotted some of the other bunks heading into the woods, but nobody was all smiling and waving. We all wanted to win.

We searched the woods for most of the morning. Sweat dripped down my back. Finally Jason and Atty called for a break and handed us each some kind of meal in an airtight bag. Mine tasted like dried-up spaghetti. Thankfully, I had the canteen Mom bought me, and I drank until it was all gone. I could fill up when we found a river.

If we found a river.

"Come on," Harper said, scooting over to where Daniel and I sat eating.

"Come on where?" Daniel said.

"Let's go make sure the . . . thing from last night . . . is safe," she said.

"Do you remember where we put it?" I asked.

"I'll know it when I see it," she said. Which meant no. We were never going to find it again.

We snuck away from the group. It wasn't like they were really going to run into the Hydra anyway. Three hours had passed and we hadn't even seen so much as a squirrel.

*That's because the Hydra ate all the squirrels,* my brain told me. I told my brain to shut up.

We circled back the way we came. I looked everywhere for the hollowed-out tree, but everything looked so different. Sunlight reflected off everything, and I wished I'd thought to put some sunscreen on. But I didn't have time to give it much thought because the most horrible sound filled my ears, like ten monsters screaming at the exact same time. We stepped forward, into a clearing.

There was the Hydra.

Daniel cowered behind a tree and looked like he was about to throw up. And Harper . . . she pulled the tiny camera thing from her pocket and started taking pictures. That left me to fight it.

"Bandanas up!" I shouted, because a disgusting stench

filled my nose. I pulled my bandana over my mouth and nose to block out the fumes. I hoped they did the same, but I didn't turn to check.

The Hydra looked like a cross between a dinosaur and a dragon that had gone wrong. It was dark red and had nine heads, all of which were bobbing around, trying to decide on the best way to eat us. For being a robot, it was amazing the way it moved, so smoothly, like nine snakes hooked together.

I raised my spear and got ready to throw it. Since the Hydra was supposed to look real, then maybe the part that controlled it was where the heart would be.

"Not the spear!" Daniel shouted just as the thing flew from my hand.

Which brought us back to how this whole thing started.

The spear hit hard, right on the Hydra's chest. Hit and bounced off. I barely had time to jump out of the way before one of the Hydra's heads lashed down and tried to make a snack of my arm. I wished that I had the shield from the Trading Post, but it was too late for that.

"What is this thing made of?" I yelled over to Daniel. Except with the yellow bandana covering my mouth, it came out a little muffled.

"Use the sword!" Daniel shouted. "Cut off its head!"

Its head. That was some kind of joke since there were nine heads. Another head darted down and tried to eat me. I rolled out of the way, through the thick red mud. This was the worst summer camp ever.

I grabbed the sword from my waist. Camp Rule Number Four said I had to carry it everywhere, and for once, I didn't disagree with the stupid rules. Not that I was some sword champion. But it couldn't be much different than swinging a baseball bat, could it?

I swung the sword, and the stupid Hydra twisted away, almost like it was doing some fun little dance.

Harper stepped in front of me. "Do you have any idea how to swing a sword?" she asked, and then she shoved me away, raised her sword, and sliced one of the heads off the Hydra.

Blood and guts spewed everywhere, drenching me, Harper, and Daniel. Which was impossible. How could a robotic Hydra monster have such realistic blood and gore?

"Nice shot," I said, wishing I'd spent more time listening when the counselors were giving us sword lessons.

I couldn't tell if she blushed since she was covered in blood.

"Not that head!" Daniel shouted.

Harper and I immediately turned to look. From the stump where the head had been, two brand new heads grew.

"Are you kidding me?" I shouted. "That is completely not fair."

The stupid thing now had ten heads, all of which were fixed on us, ready to tear us to shreds.

Daniel looked at me and Harper like we'd forgotten our brains at home. "Don't you guys know anything about the Hydra?"

"No!" I said. "Remember the part where I said I didn't know anything about mythology? And why is this thing bleeding? It's not real."

"It is real!" Daniel shouted. "And you have to cut off the mortal head."

The mortal head! That was crazy. I had no clue what the mortal head was. Another head twisted and struck at me. I jumped to the side, barely getting out of the way.

"How do I know which one is the mortal head?" I yelled.

Harper stayed where she was, swinging the sword just to keep the thing away.

"I don't know," Daniel said.

That wasn't the right answer.

"Run!" I yelled, and we took off, through the trees. My feet pounded the ground, and I didn't dare look back. Every step I took, I tried to pretend that the entire thing wasn't real, but my mind was done making excuses.

When we finally found the rest of our bunk, I leaned against a tree and sank to the ground. There was no sign of the Hydra.

"It's real," I said. "It's all real."

Jason patted me on the shoulder. "Of course it is, Logan."

I wished he was joking but I knew he wasn't. Everything about this camp was real, including the part where, if we weren't careful, we could die.

"Can you show us where it is?" Atty said.

"Oh, I can," Daniel said, and he led the way, back through the woods, to the clearing.

There was no sign of the Hydra. But the blood and guts and severed head were still there on the red muddy ground.

Jason picked up the head and studied it, then tossed it back to the ground. "It's not the mortal head."

"No kidding," I said. "We cut it off and two more grew in its place."

"You mean I cut it off," Harper said.

"Whatever," I said.

"If we found it once, we can find it again," Jason said, and for the next five hours, we scoured the woods, searching everywhere. We saw three of the other bunks, a couple deer running by, some cows going to the bathroom, but no Hydra.

We stumbled back to camp around five o'clock. Most of the other bunks were there already. I thought being covered in Hydra blood was bad, but one of the bunks, Team Cow Stable they called themselves, were covered in dung. I smelled it the second we were within fifty feet of them.

Hercules was just coming down from Mount Olympus, in his leather pants and gold sequin shirt. Of course, he wasn't carrying the amphora, since we'd stolen it. He motioned for everyone to be quiet, and then put on his best serious face. He'd probably practiced it in front of the mirror.

"It's a sad day here at Camp Hercules," Hercules said. "For safety reasons, we're going to have to call off the hunts until certain matters can be resolved."

Call off the hunts. That would have been good to know before we almost got killed by the Hydra. Everyone started talking at once.

But just then, the final bunk came back. It was Achilles' bunk, Team Three-headed Dog, or something like that. They looked like they'd turned into zombies because they were all super pale and covered in gore. But that wasn't what anyone was looking at. What we were all staring at was the giant dog they pulled behind them on a chain. The giant dog with three heads.

# CHAPTER 14

Achilles sauntered up to the center of camp, right by Lucky Rock. Like his bunk, he was so pale that he looked like he'd been dipped in powdered sugar and covered in fake blood, like something from a Halloween haunted house.

"Team Cerberus has completed its labor," he said. The smug look on his face was unbelievable. As if he didn't already think his team was the best. He would never let any of the rest of us live this down.

Jason threw his shield to the ground and looked like he wanted to spit on Achilles.

Helen, his co-counselor, walked up beside him. "I assume we're first?" she said, tossing her hair over her shoulder.

"No!" Hercules said. "We can't do the labors right now!"

Confusion clouded both Achilles' and Helen's faces.

"Look, is this because of the bet I made with Theseus?" Achilles said. "Because it's totally legit. Nothing in the rules says we can't make side bets."

"It's not that," Hercules said. "You have to put him back."

Team Three-headed Dog walked forward, pulling the creature along with them.

"There is no way we're putting Cerberus back," one of the guys in their bunk said. I think his name was Ryan.

"Yeah, no way," one of the girls said. I knew her name since she was super cute (though she always seemed to be scowling). Amelia. "You would not believe what we had to go through to capture him. Do you think I like being covered in guts?"

I knew I didn't.

"Put. Him. Back!" Hercules hollered. There was no mistaking his tone. He was not kidding.

This finally seemed to register on Achilles. He glanced to Lucky Rock, to where the amphora should be, and seemed to realize that it wasn't there.

"Oh no, the curse . . . ," Achilles said. Then he turned back to his team. "We need to—"

He never got the chance to finish. The giant three-headed dog, Cerberus, reared up onto its hind legs, yanking the chain from Ryan's and Amelia's grasps. It started running a circle around camp, scattering kids everywhere.

Hercules jumped into its path, trying to stop it, but the dog jumped right over him. Then it took off, for the woods, dragging the chain behind it. Everyone was screaming and shouting and running around, and the entire camp was chaos. I ended up pressed up against the flagpole, the flag of Camp Hercules waving in the wind. I don't think this was how the day was supposed to go.

"Campers!" Hercules shouted, standing on Lucky Rock. "We have a new mission. Capture Cerberus and return him to the Underworld." Then he took off running, back up the slopes of Mount Olympus.

Jason and Atty gathered us in a circle.

"Okay, Team Hydra, here's what we need to do," Atty said. "We split up and find Cerberus. If you find him, you send one person to get Jason and me, and we'll take him back to the Underworld. We're demigods, so we can. You can't. Got it?"

She did that thing with her eyes again, fixing them on each of us, daring us to disagree with her.

"Got it," we all said. Like anyone was going to argue with Atty.

The other bunks were all doing the same as us. A couple started heading for the woods. I was itching to go, because how awesome would it be to be the guy who saved the day? I could almost see myself wrestling the giant three-headed dog to the ground.

"Why can't Hercules catch Cerberus?" Daniel said, pulling me from my daydream.

He had a really good point. If Hercules were really—like really—Hercules, then shouldn't he be able to do any of these labors all by himself?

"Hercules has something else he needs to take care of," Jason said, and even though he didn't say it, I knew he was talking about finding the amphora.

"Jason and I will be in the clearing where Harper, Daniel, and Logan fought the Hydra," Atty said. "Immediately come get us when you find him. Don't do anything else. Got it?"

"Got it," we all said at the same time.

I was ready to go.

"Come on," I said, motioning for Daniel and Harper to follow. We ran for the trees, but the second we passed into the forest, we stopped dead in our tracks.

There were the three creepy old ladies standing in the middle of the path. Their gray hair was spiked up and they still wore the sunglasses. They had their black leather pants on and tank tops that matched the colored streaks in their hair.

"Fifteen minutes, Sugar Plum," the lady in the middle

with the yellow streak in her hair said. She held the green ball of yarn, and stared right at me. At least it looked like she was staring right at me. With the dark sunglasses on, it was impossible to tell where she was looking.

I stared her down. "What about fifteen minutes?"

"For fifteen minutes off your life, we'll tell you where Cerberus is, Darling," the lady on the left with the red streak said.

Fifteen minutes off my life! These ladies were completely crazy. Except what if they weren't?

"They're the Fates," Daniel whispered next to me.

"What does that mean?" I asked.

"It means they really can take time off your life," Harper said.

"You mean you really gave them five minutes of your life for a toothbrush?" I said to Daniel.

He shrugged. "No cavities. Ever. That means I never have to visit the dentist again."

He had a good point. I made a mental note to visit the Trading Post once this whole Cerberus mess was over and get myself a new toothbrush.

If the women cared that we were talking about them, they didn't show it. They just stood there waiting.

"Do we have a deal, Buttercup?" the lady on the right with the blue streak in her hair said. She held the giant scissors next to the yarn.

I immediately wanted to say no, because who in their right mind would ever agree to something like that? Except then, images of dragging Cerberus to the Underworld all by myself filled my mind. I would be a hero. The best in camp. Even Hercules would know my name.

"Fine," I said. "It's a deal."

The lady on the left held the iPad out, and I touched the giant eyeball on the screen. It lit up green. Then the lady on the right used the giant scissors to cut off a piece of the yarn.

Harper smacked my arm. "No, Logan!"

"Too late," the lady on the right said.

"Tell me now," I said. It may have been a stupid deal to make, but it was done. I wanted my answer.

Images filled my mind, of Cerberus, drinking water with all three of his tongues out of a river, and I knew where he was. But the images continued on, showing me a cave that led downward. It was the Underworld, where he needed to go. And I was the one leading him, not Jason and not Atty.

"Got it," I said. "Let's go."

# CHAPTER 15

**I**f you really know where Cerberus is, we should go get Jason and Atty," Daniel said.

I shook my head. "Let's just go find him. See if I'm right." Not that I needed to see to know. There was no doubt in my mind. I knew where to find the creek, and I knew Cerberus would be there. I also knew I could take him to the Underworld myself, demigod or not.

Daniel was not convinced. "I'm not sure that's a good idea. What do you think, Harper?"

She had the pen camera clasped tightly in her hand, and any time she saw anything out of the ordinary, she snapped a picture of it. "I agree with Logan," she said. "We should go see. I mean, what if he's wrong? Atty would probably shave our heads, she'd be so mad."

I knew I should step back and think about how mad they'd

be if we captured Cerberus without them, but I couldn't get the image of being a hero out of my mind. I'd never dreamed of being a hero, but now it was all I could think about.

"Logan," Daniel said, breaking me from my thoughts.

"What?"

"Are we going to go get Jason and Atty?"

I shook my head. "No. We're not."

I led the way through the trees, ducking under limbs and cutting through paths that were completely hidden. But I knew they were there. The Fates had shown me exactly where I needed to go.

What they hadn't told me was how ginormous Cerberus really was. He was as tall as a horse and about as wide as Mom's car. He was also exactly where the Fates had said he would be. All three of his heads were lapping up water from the creek. It bubbled and flowed over rocks, brimming to the top, which was impossible given the drought we'd been having in Austin for that last month. Of course a three-headed dog was also impossible. So yeah, all the water hardly even fazed me.

"What is it with mythology and things having more than one head?" I said. Like seriously, the Hydra had nine heads—well ten, since Harper had cut off one and two more had grown back. And Cerberus had three heads. Why does a dog need three heads?

I guess I spoke too loud, because one of his heads lifted up from the water and looked directly at us. Harper started taking pictures.

"We need to go get Jason!" Daniel said, not even trying

to be quiet.

The other two heads lifted up and looked our way.

"We don't have time!" Even if I hadn't had the visions of being a hero, I was still right about this. Cerberus could probably eat all three of us before we made it a single tree's distance.

"Oh no! Oh no! Oh no!" Daniel said, and he squeezed his eyes shut, like that would make the entire thing go away.

But Harper took a step closer to get a better angle for her pictures. "Do you see the size of his mouths?"

"I'm trying not to," Daniel said.

I whipped around to face him. "How did Hercules ever capture Cerberus?" I asked.

"I don't know," Daniel said, but he was so scared, I don't think he even heard me.

I grabbed his shoulders and looked him right in the eyes. "Focus, Daniel. How did Hercules capture Cerberus?"

Daniel took a few deep breaths to calm himself. Either that or he was hyperventilating. "He wrestled him with his strength. That's how. It's because Hercules was so strong."

I glanced back at Cerberus. Even the three of us together weren't going to be able to capture the dog monster by wrestling him. Cerberus was still watching us and hadn't come any closer. Maybe because he realized we were completely incapable of capturing him. Except Team Cerberus had done it, so there had to be a way.

"He's a dog, right?" I asked.

Focusing on factual questions seemed to have a calming effect of Daniel. He nodded. "Yeah, I mean he's a monster, but he's still a dog."

"Okay, and what do dogs like?" I asked aloud, even as my mind went over it. I didn't have a dog, but some of my friends did. Dogs loved treats, but I didn't have any food on me right now. Dogs loved playing fetch, not that I thought that would help us since we wanted to capture him, not make him run away. Oh, and dogs loved . . .

"Tummy rubs!" I said.

"You're going to give Cerberus a tummy rub?" Daniel said.

"Good idea," Harper said. "Come here, puppy." She put her hand down low and took a step toward the dog.

Cerberus growled with his center head.

"That's okay," Harper said. "We're not going to hurt you."

"Right," I said. "We're gonna take you home, to the Underworld."

At the word 'home,' the ears on all three of Cerberus' heads perked up. Then his tail started wagging. Harper took another step forward. And then another. She was almost in reaching distance, which meant she was either about to give Cerberus a monster tummy rub, or she was going to get her hand bitten off.

"Who's a good dog?" Harper said. "Who is?"

And that was all Cerberus could take. He flopped over, onto his back and exposed his tummy. Harper started rubbing his stomach, and his back leg started twitching. I took the opportunity to grab the end of the chain that was still looped around his neck.

"Good dog," Harper said. "Come on, Daniel. Don't be so scared."

"I'm fine back here," Daniel said. "You know, maybe I should go get Jason and Atty now?"

"No time," I said. "Who's ready to go home?"

Cerberus jumped to his feet and barked with all three heads. They each had a distinct barking sound. The one in the center was deep and scary. The one on the left was excited, like it wanted to jump up and down and fetch a ball. And the one on the right was super squeaky, like a Chihuahua.

"Let's go." I started down the side of the creek, and Cerberus following, prancing, like we were on some great adventure. Now as long as the location of the Underworld was where the Fates said it would be, we'd be set. We could dump Cerberus off and be done.

The creek curved around the side of another mountain. Well, maybe not a mountain, since it was nowhere near as big as Mount Olympus, but it was good-sized hill. And tucked under a rock ledge and hidden behind some trees, was the opening to a cave. Bats flew around the entrance, making horrible, screeching noises.

We stepped in front of the cave, and immediately waves of heat pulsed over us. Moans of what sounded like people dying or in horrible pain floated across the air.

I was pretty sure my face was exactly like Harper's and Daniel's. There was no part of me that wanted to go any closer to the cave.

"Here you are, boy," I said, unlooping the chain from Cerberus' neck. I could bring it back as proof that we'd completed the mission.

Cerberus jumped up and down and barked, the excited bark. But he didn't go into the cave. Instead he kept turning to us and then back at that cave. I grabbed a stick and threw it into the cave. Cerberus whined, like he wanted to fetch it, but he didn't move.

"No way," Daniel said. "I am not going in there."

Maybe Cerberus understood English, because then he let out the deep scary bark, and he edged closer to Daniel.

"Please don't let him eat me," Daniel said. "Please. Please. Please."

Cerberus grabbed hold of the side of Daniel's yellow camp T-shirt with his teeth and started pulling him toward the cave. The message was pretty clear. Either we were taking him all the way home, or he was going to snack on us for dinner. It was an easy choice.

We were going into the Underworld.

# CHAPTER 16

"**I**t smells awful in here," Harper said. She plugged her nose and curled her lip in disgust.

Not that I could blame her. The stench was overwhelming, and each step we took, it got worse. Cerberus loved it though. He kept stopping and rolling over on the dirt floor, like he was trying to get as much bat poop on himself as possible. Bats kept dive-bombing at our hair. I swatted them away.

"This is such a bad idea," Daniel said. "Like the worst idea you've ever had in your life, Logan. Even worse than that time in first grade you dared me to race you to the top of the jungle gym."

I filed through my memories, but nothing about a jungle gym came up. "I have no idea what you're talking about."

The fear slipped off Daniel's face and was replaced by

disbelief. "Are you kidding me? You said I couldn't climb to the top. You dared me to do it."

"Okay," I said. "So did you?" It still wasn't coming back to me.

"Yeah, I did," Daniel said. "And I fell and broke my arm. You don't remember that?"

Harper looked at me like I was an insensitive moron, so I tried again to remember. And there was this little nagging memory tucked away in the corner of my mind. Of Daniel sitting in the gravel at the elementary school playground crying and holding his arm. Waves of guilt rolled over me. They were the exact same waves I'd felt at the time. But I also remembered that at the time, I'd felt so bad that I'd tried to pretend it wasn't a big deal.

"I was a real jerk, wasn't I?" I said.

Daniel didn't say anything.

"I'm sorry," I said. "I didn't think you'd fall."

"Well, I did," Daniel said, crossing his arms. "I had that stupid cast on for the entire summer, in Texas. Do you know how hot a cast is during the summer in Texas? And when you get an itch . . . well, it's the worst."

Harper glared at me like I was a demon now.

"Look, I'm really sorry," I said. "But this isn't a bad idea, like that was. This is something we have to do."

Almost like he understood what we were saying, Cerberus barked three times, really quickly, and then tried to get us to keep walking.

"How do you know?" Daniel said.

I blew out a deep breath, and even though it was going

to make me sound as crazy as everyone else at this camp, I said, "The Fates told me. And I feel like we should listen to the Fates."

Daniel didn't say anything for ten seconds, but then he nodded. "Okay. That works for me."

Maybe my apology had worked. Or maybe it was because I'd finally accepted his messed up world of mythology as truth.

We kept walking, down the long cave, ducking to get out of the path of the bats. Every second, it got steeper and smellier, like we were walking into a sewer. Harper pulled the bandana over her nose and mouth, and I did the same. It worked both against poisonous Hydra fumes and smelly Underworld stenches. I was about to ask what Daniel and Harper thought was smelling so bad, when the tunnel finally leveled out and torches lit up the underground cavern. Then I saw for myself.

Ahead of us stretched a black river, so dark and thick, it looked like someone had taken black paint and dumped it in a bowl and let it sit. Except floating on the surface were all sorts of things that looked dead, like animals and trees and . . . I didn't want my mind to go any further than that. It was just gross. And smelled really bad.

Cerberus ran to the edge of the water and started drinking from it with all three of his heads. I almost lost my dehydrated spaghetti, but managed to keep it down—barely. But how could he drink that stuff? Seriously? I was so focused on watching him (or trying to not watch him) that I didn't even notice the black wooden boat pull up to the shore.

This guy got out and walked toward us. He wore black jeans, a black T-shirt, and a black knit hat.

Daniel's mouth dropped open.

"You're not . . . ," Daniel said.

"Charon?" the guy said. "Yep. In the flesh. Well, not really flesh. I mean, technically flesh, but things get kind of confusing here in the Underworld since so many things are dead."

Things that were floating in the water.

Daniel stepped back. "Uh huh."

"We brought Cerberus back," Harper said. And then she pulled out the little pen camera and started taking pictures of everything around her: the water, the boat, and even the creepy Charon guy.

"Let me see that," Charon said, and he held a hand out to her.

Harper's face froze. It looked like the last thing she wanted to do was give him the camera. She seemed to fight it with every bit of her willpower. But she ended up placing it right into his outstretched palm.

Charon looked at it and tilted his head like he was trying to figure out what it was. "So you're a spy?" he said.

"No. Not a spy," Harper said. "I'm an investigative reporter." She tried to act all proud when she said this.

Charon nodded, and then threw the camera over his shoulder into the black, disgusting water. It sat on the surface and then slowly disappeared underneath.

"You can't do that," Harper said.

Charon acted like he was confused. "But I just did."

"That's not fair," Harper said. "I want to talk to your boss."

Charon stepped to the side and motioned to the boat. "Sure. I'll take you over to talk to Hades. But you can't come back."

"Ha ha," Harper said, starting for the boat.

Daniel grabbed her arm. "He's not kidding. Anyone who goes to the Underworld can't return."

Harper bit her lip. "But my pictures. My mom is counting on me to get her information."

"What?" I said. "Are you kidding? You are spying? For your mom?"

"It's not spying," Harper said. "It's investigative reporting. My mom was sure something was up with this camp, and the pictures prove it." She'd managed to shrug off Daniel and kept looking to the boat, like she was trying to decide if it was worth it.

Spy or not, I couldn't let Harper get stuck in the Underworld forever.

"We need to get back," I said. "We can find you other proof."

Harper scowled, mostly at Charon since he was the one who threw away her camera.

"Fine," she said. "But just for the record, I'm filing an official complaint."

"I wouldn't get on my bad side," Charon said. "Just some advice." He stared for a really long time, right at Harper, almost like they were talking back and forth in their minds.

Then he headed back to the boat. Cerberus jumped in beside him and hung his heads over the side as Charon pushed the boat away from shore.

# CHAPTER 17

"**A**re you crazy?" Daniel said. "You don't mess with gods of the Underworld." We hurried away from the Underworld, back up the long path we'd come.

"Did you see what that guy did though?" Harper said. "He threw away my camera. My mom is going to be furious."

"Yeah, well, your mom being mad is nothing compared to the god of the Underworld getting mad," Daniel said. "You know he's going to tell Hades. And then Hades—"

I put up my hand to stop them. This was getting out of control. "Can we just get back to camp? We'll show them the chain and tell them that we captured Cerberus and took him back."

Since my logic was perfect, neither of them could argue with it. We hurried the rest of the way back above ground in silence. I think Harper was still annoyed about her camera and Daniel was still freaked out over the Underworld. I'll be the first to admit, when my feet hit the open air, I let out a breath I might have been holding the entire time. Gods and three-headed dogs and the Underworld complete with dead things floating in the black water!

I grabbed the chain from next to the tree where I'd left it. "You know I wanted to go to football camp," I said.

"Football camp!" Harper said. "And you think that would have been more fun?"

I thought about it for a second, going over everything that had happened so far, just in the week since we'd been here. Making weapons. Climbing Mount Olympus. Stealing the amphora from the harpy guard. Capturing a three-headed dog. Sure, I couldn't tell any of my friends about it when I got back since they'd never believe me, but it all was pretty epic.

"No, probably not," I said. "But I think it should be mentioned that I didn't want to be here in the first place."

We headed back for camp, me leading the way since the whole map that the Fates had planted in my head was still in place. Those Fates were pretty helpful. I'll give them that.

*One day*, a voice in my head seemed to say. *Kill the Hydra for one day off your life.*

Images of the Hydra came to me, just like the images that they'd sent of Cerberus.

But an entire day? I couldn't let the time keep adding up. What if I was about to have my most glorious moment ever, and then time got cut short?

I ignored the voice, and we hurried the rest of the way

back to the clearing in the woods. Everyone from our bunk, including Jason and Atty, were there, pacing. They all turned to look.

"Where have you three been?" Jason said. He looked ready to rip the hair from our scalps. "You've been gone for hours."

"Hours?" Harper said. "We've been gone for like a half hour at the most."

Atty shook her head, and her laser eyes bore into us. "Half hour!" She laughed. "We've sent out search parties. There was no sign of you."

I dropped the chain to the red mud beneath our feet. It landed with a solid thud, and immediately relief from not carting the thing around moved through my arm. "We captured Cerberus. And returned him to the Underworld."

Atty's eyes got so big, I thought they might fall out of her head. "You what?"

"Captured Cerberus," I said. I noticed Daniel slink behind me, like he was trying to hide.

"You were supposed to come find us," Jason said.

I shook my head. "There was no time." And I gave them a shortened account of everything that had happened, leaving out the part about the Fates. I also left out the part about Charon taking Harper's camera away since she probably didn't want everyone to know she was a spy. At the story of our heroics, I fully expected everyone to start cheering. That's not what happened at all.

"Bunk chores for two weeks," Jason said. He threw his spear, sticking it into a nearby tree.

"Two weeks!" Daniel said. "I didn't even want to go. I shouldn't have to do extra chores."

But his excuses were about as useful as my protests. Here, we'd saved the day. We'd returned the monster dog to the Underworld. And the only reward we were getting was extra toilet scrubbing duty.

"Fine," I said. "So that solves the camp's problem, right?"

"Hardly," Jason said. "Pack up. We're heading back to base camp."

He and Atty were grouchy and wouldn't talk the entire time we walked back to Lucky Rock. But the rest of our bunkmates kept hanging back, asking us what it was like and how we did it. And sure, it wasn't the hero worship that I'd quite imagined when the Fates had given me the images, but it did make me feel like a rock star.

All that changed when we got back to Lucky Rock. Jason and Atty hurried over to Hercules and filled him in on what had happened. He kept glancing over and glaring at us. The rest of the bunks were already back. Word spread among them, and most everyone seemed chill about the whole thing. Everyone except the campers in Achilles' bunk: Team Cerberus. They were still ghost white and covered in gore, but now they had sour looks plastered on their faces.

"You should have let us capture Cerberus," the guy named Ryan said. He shook his head, getting little bits of blood and goop on me.

I didn't even flinch. "You should have found him first."

"I'll remember this, Team Hydra," Ryan said, and then stomped off, back to his bunkmates.

Jason and Atty hurried back to join our bunk, and Hercules jumped up on Lucky Rock. He raised his arms like he was trying to quiet us down, but it also looked like he was working really hard to flex his muscles. They rippled under his tank top and the sun reflected off them.

"Campers, we have a bigger problem than Cerberus, and I can no longer try to hide it from you," Hercules said. "Our amphora has been stolen."

A hush went over our group. I tried to act really surprised, like it was the first I'd heard of it.

"Without the amphora, camp can't operate," Hercules said.

"Why not?" someone asked. It was a girl with long dark hair that she had tied back into a ponytail.

Hercules pressed his thumb and forefinger to the bridge of his nose, like this entire situation pained him beyond belief. "The amphora is not just symbolic, like you might think. It is actually the source of the power of camp. It controls the labors. It brings them all here."

Daniel's mouth fell open, like he was trying to process all of this. Maybe I was, too.

Since I was still feeling all brave from my recent victory, I got up the courage to ask a question. "So the amphora is like a magic thing that makes the mythology real?"

Hercules gritted his teeth. "The mythology is real. It controls the curse."

"What curse?" I asked. Jason looked like he was about to punch me if I didn't shut up. But come on. A curse and real magic. What was going on at this camp anyway?

96

Hercules shook his head. "A curse thanks to my step-mother Hera. It started out with twelve labors. I'm sure you all know about those or you wouldn't be here."

I nodded even though I'd never heard of them before camp. But whatever.

"I completed the labors in record time," Hercules said. "And this infuriated Hera. She placed a curse on me. That I would have to repeat the labors over and over for all of eternity. Which I did, many, many times. But then I had a brilliant idea. I would capture all the labors and store them in the amphora. And then, wherever I brought the amphora, the labors would be. So I created Camp Hercules—it's a pretty catchy name, I know—so you campers would be able to share in the glory of my labors."

"You want us to do your dirty work," I said.

"I thought it would be fun for you," Hercules said. "For many generations of kids. I enjoyed it the first one hundred or so times I did it. After all, who wouldn't want to fight monsters? But without the amphora, none of the labors can be controlled. We need to find it."

Harper stepped forward, and I was sure she was about to tell everyone how we'd stolen the amphora. And how we could find it—maybe—and bring it back. But instead, she said, "Do you know who stole it?"

Hercules took a deep breath, way over exaggerated if you ask me. "I believe it is the work of Hera or one of her minions. Possibly one of you, working for Hera."

Wait! Was Harper working for Hera?

I looked to her, and almost like she knew what I was

thinking, she shook her head. But that didn't mean anything.

"The good news is this," Hercules said. "The labors are still here, within the walls of Camp Hercules. Which means the amphora is still here, too. We just need to find it."

"Wait!" someone cried. It was a kid from Team Cow Stable stumbling toward camp, covered in cow poop. "I found it!" he shouted.

He grasped the amphora with both hands, and was running toward us.

"Hera," Hercules said, and a huge grin covered his face. "Your plans have been foiled." He sounded like some cheesy superhero from an old-time action movie.

"Someone stuffed it in a tree," the Team Cow Stable kid said. "And the tree almost didn't let me get it. It came alive and tried to swallow me. But I fought it off. I got it!"

He ran the rest of the way, ready to deliver the amphora right into Hercules' hands. Except he wasn't looking down, not even as he tripped on Lucky Rock.

The amphora flew from his hands, straight up. Hercules and every single counselor ran for it, trying to catch it. But it did not want to be caught. Instead it vaulted upward and then came down, smashing on Lucky Rock.

Nobody moved. Nobody said a word. Then the world around us came to life. The stomping of one thousand bulls' hooves. The snarl of the giant boar. The scream of the Hydra's ten heads.

"Take cover!" Hercules shouted. He grabbed his sword and leapt onto Lucky Rock, like he was going to protect all of us. Jason and Atty herded us into the dining hall, along with the eleven other bunks. They'd barely shut the door when something slammed into it.

The giant boar. It backed up and ran for the door again. And again. The walls around us shook.

"What does this mean?" Daniel said.

Atty pulled the sword from its scabbard and held it in front of her. Then she turned to face us.

"It means that Hercules has lost control of the labors," Atty said. "And if we don't do something about it, we're all going to die."

⇥⇤

# CHAPTER 18

I braced the front door of the dining hall, putting all my weight behind it. This was a huge mistake. The boar slammed into the door, and all ten of us who were pushing against it flew backward, halfway to the chicken nuggets aisle. I landed on my butt which would have been embarrassing except we were all about to die.

The boar slammed into the door again, knocking ten more campers over. Ten more ran to hold it. This is what we'd been doing for the last hour: taking turns getting thrown across the room.

"Get up!" Harper screamed, grabbing my arms and dragging me to my feet.

I jumped up and ran back for the door. Daniel was next to me, holding his sword upside down. But now wasn't the time for sword lessons so I didn't correct him.

"Do you think it will ever get tired?" I asked. I sure was. The giant boar might be a creature from mythology, but it should still need to rest.

"It's going to stop," Daniel said. "Any minute now."

He acted like he knew what he was talking about, and a lot of the time he did, but I didn't think now was one of those times. He may have read tons of stuff on mythology, but reading about monsters was a lot different than fighting them.

I prepared myself for another impact, but the sound of thunder filled the air. It started low, almost like rumbling way far away, but every second it got louder. So loud that the walls and ceiling of the dining hall started shaking. Small statues of Hercules toppled from the pedestals where they were displayed, and the tables and chairs rattled and bounced around.

The boar must've heard it too, because it stopped its charge two feet away from the door and turned to look behind it. Then it tucked its curly tail between its legs and bolted, leaving a perfect view of the mob of creatures galloping right for us.

"It's the Horses of Diomedes!" Atty shouted.

Horses didn't quite describe what was headed right for us. More like fire-breathing, man-eating monsters that happened to resemble horses in that they had four legs, a snout, and a mane of thick hair. That was about as far as the resemblance went. These were not horses like they had at the state fair. The closer they got, the more the walls shook around us.

"Brace the columns!" Jason yelled, and he ran for one of the giant stone columns that held up the ceiling. The problem was that there were at least twenty columns in the dining hall and only just over a hundred campers.

Harper, Daniel, and I ran for the nearest column. I wrapped my arms around it to hold it steady. My teeth rattled together. It felt like the rumbling went on forever as the horses got closer. And closer. I was sure they were going to run right into the door. They got so close that their thick horse hair brushed against the windows. But then they veered off and ran back the way they came.

"That was close," Jason said, running his hands over the column to make sure it was steady.

"But they're gone, right?" I said. Horses already weren't my favorite things in the world. Giant horses that could trample me with a single step were even worse.

Atty glared at me. "For now, Logan," she said. "But don't you dare assume they won't be back. Because if you do, and if they catch you, they will eat you alive, one bite at a time."

Atty had a perfect way of making horrible things seem even worse than they already were.

"You've seen that happen?" Harper asked.

I couldn't believe she was challenging Atty.

Atty leaned down and looked Harper right in the eye. "Only once. That was enough. Don't let it happen to you."

We were all so focused on the front door that we jumped when something kicked the back door. It rattled and sawdust fell from where the hinges were screwed in. Then it kicked it again. And again.

I ran to a window and looked out.

"It's a giant cow bull thing!" I shouted.

Too loud.

The bull had been kicking at the door, but it must've heard me because it bolted over to the window where I was looking out and smashed the glass with one of its horns. The horn came way too close to my face.

I jumped back, but not before the bull snorted directly at me. Huge chunks of bull boogers flew from its nostrils and covered me.

"Gross!" I shouted.

"Stop your complaining," Atty said. She pushed me out of the way and ran for the window, her spear gripped tightly in her hand. Then she poked the spear through the window.

The bull ran off, toward the trees.

"Did you get it?" Daniel asked.

Atty whipped around to face us. "No. I didn't get it. It'll be back, just like all the labors. And where is Hercules? We need an update."

"He's coming!" Achilles shouted. "Open the front door!"

Five of the counselors ran over and lifted the huge metal bar holding the door closed. Hercules ran in, and they slammed it closed behind him.

"What's the status?" Jason said. He gripped his shield and sword and hadn't even broken a sweat. I think he and some of the other demigod counselors could have gone on fighting these monsters forever, but I was beat.

Hercules walked to the center of the dining hall, brushing off his leather pants and gold sequined top. He hopped up onto a table and flexed his muscles like he always did.

"The situation is not good," Hercules said. "It—"

He never got a chance to finish his sentence because an arrow flew in through the broken window and buried itself in his leg.

 **CHAPTER 19**

**"I**t's the Amazons!" Jason shouted.

All twenty-four counselors jumped into action. They pushed us together and surrounded us, lifting their shields to protect us. More arrows flew in through the windows. I glanced outside.

"What are those?" I shouted over the noise. As if everything I'd seen in the last week wasn't unbelievable enough, there were a bunch of women wearing animal skins riding horses outside. They had bows and arrows and spears and shields, and they kept shouting and yelling like we were in full-out war.

With them! For no reason!

Daniel grabbed me and pulled me out of line of the window. "They're Amazons."

"What are Amazons?" I asked.

"Fierce warrior women," Harper said. I swear she almost said it with an edge of pride in her voice, like she wanted to be out there with them.

"Why are they firing at Hercules?" I couldn't imagine that one of Hercules' twelve labors had anything to do with these women. They were scary, but they weren't monsters. Unless they turned into monsters when it got dark out, like werewolves or something. After coming to Camp Hercules, nothing would surprise me when it came to mythology.

Hercules was still on the table, but a few of the demigod counselors had him shielded. He wrapped his hand around the arrow in his thigh and yanked it out. I cringed. He didn't even grimace. It was bad enough when I got cactus splinters in my finger and Mom had to pull them out with tweezers. I couldn't imagine yanking an arrow out of my leg.

Oh, right. This was Hercules. Strongest guy in the world. If I had any doubt of this before, watching him break the arrow in half and throw it at the Amazon women made my doubts go away. I couldn't believe anyone messed with Hercules. Not Amazons. Not monsters. Not even his crazy goddess stepmother Hera.

"He's trying to steal a belt from them," Daniel said.

"A belt? They're trying to kill him because he's trying to steal a belt?" That made no sense at all.

"It's a special belt," Harper said. "Their leader, Hippolyta wears it. It's like a superhero utility belt, with all her weapons and stuff stored inside."

"It's one of his labors," Daniel said.

Right. So stealing a belt was one of the labors. Even

if it did make her kind of a superhero like Batman, it still seemed a little weird. Of course every single thing about this camp was weird. The warrior women just happened to be the weirdest thing in the last hour.

The women let out some sort of synchronized yell. It started with one of them—she did have a pretty fancy belt, all made of gold and covered with white gems—and passed down the line, until every single Amazon was making the sound. Then they parted, making a giant path in the middle of their group.

I just had time to see a thousand cows coming down the path before Achilles and Theseus covered the window. It sounded like a monster truck rally outside as the cows got closer.

"This is not going to be pretty," Jason said. I figured the cows were going to stampede right into the dining hall, but he didn't order anyone to brace the door or anything like that.

The pounding of the cows' hooves stopped, and then the most gods-awful stench filled the dining hall. Darkness began to cover the door, sealing out the little bits of light that were coming through. Once the door was completely covered, the cows stampeded off, leaving their stench behind.

"What is that smell?" I said.

Atty patted my shoulder. "Logan, you do not want to know."

Daniel leaned over and whispered, "It's the Augean Cows."

The kids in Team Cow Stable shrank back, like they were afraid Hercules was going to make them go out there and clean the mess up right now. They were still covered in cow dung from earlier.

Hercules stomped his foot on the table, and everyone got really quiet again. I plugged my nose because I'm not going to lie. The smell could have made me pass out on the spot. And then I remembered my bandana. I pulled it over my mouth and nose, and instantly relief flooded through me.

A lot of the other campers did the same with their bandanas. Not all. Maybe those kids were trying to be like the demigods and act like they didn't need to block out the stench. But I wasn't too proud.

"Campers, as you can see, the situation is out of control," Hercules said. "I've been out there all day, trying to control the labors, but all at once, they are too much, even for me."

A bunch of kids started shouting that no way was anything too much for Hercules. He motioned for them to be quiet.

"What this means is that I need your help now more than ever," Hercules said. "I am counting on each and every one of you."

"What do you need us to do?" Ryan from Team Cerberus asked. He stood all tall in his blue camp T-shirt, and I swear he puffed his chest out, trying to act like he was a mini-Hercules or something.

"I could totally take him," I whispered to Daniel and Harper.

Harper rolled her eyes and didn't say a word, but Daniel said, "You think so?"

"Totally."

Maybe I said it too loud, because Atty gave me one of her death stares.

"I need two things from each of you," Hercules said. "That is all. Two simple little things."

Simple. Right. Like I believed that.

"First," Hercules said. "I am one hundred percent certain that there is a spy for Hera among us." His eyes scanned our group of campers. "I don't know who the spy is, but I am sure that at least one exists. This spy is responsible for stealing the amphora and possibly orchestrating its destruction."

"I swear I tripped!" Will from Team Cow Stable said. He'd been the one who'd found the amphora in the woods.

"So the story goes," Hercules said. "But what forces made you trip?"

I was willing to bet that Will was just clumsy. He was tall and skinny and his feet were huge. He probably tripped on everything.

Will shrank back under the question. "Hera?" he said, hesitantly.

"Yes, Hera," Hercules said. "She is the force behind it all."

I leaned over to Harper. "You should tell him," I said in barely a whisper.

Harper gave the smallest shake of her head. And I get that she didn't want to tell Hercules that she'd been the one to steal the amphora.

Okay, fine, all three of us stole it. But it had been her idea, so I held her mostly to blame. Still, if we didn't tell Hercules, he was going to go on believing this 'Spy of Hera' stuff.

"Your first task, campers, is to look for this spy," Hercules said. "As long as the spy is unknown, Camp Hercules is not safe."

With giant boars and flesh-eating horses and Amazon warrior women, Camp Hercules had never been safe. But now was not the time to point that out.

"And second," Hercules said. "I cannot handle these labors alone. Not all at once, as our current situation demands. This means that we are all going to need to work together to defeat the labors. Each team is responsible for its labor. We cannot hide any longer."

That was totally fine by me. I was ready for my rematch against the Hydra.

The counselors jumped into action, each setting up a home base in the dining hall.

"Team Hydra, with us," Jason shouted. He and Atty stood near the pizza aisle. If only they'd been serving pizza right now. With all the fighting from today, I'd worked up a serious appetite.

We hurried over and circled round. Atty slammed a giant map of Camp Hercules on the ground in front of us. The gold fence could be seen as a solid line around camp. She traced her finger around it.

"This right here is the only thing keeping the rest of the world safe from the labors," Atty said. "This fence. And this gate."

She pointed at the gate where Mom had dropped me off a week ago. It had been a seriously crazy week. Mom would be furious if she knew what was really going on at this camp.

She should have sent me to football camp instead.

"We need to make sure the gate stays closed," Jason said. "If you see anyone near the gate, you need to report it to us immediately."

We all nodded.

"What about the Hydra?" Daniel said. "How are we going to defeat it?"

Jason and Atty looked at each other and nodded. "We have a plan for that." But their next words got lost as the thunderous horse hooves returned. The walls and columns started to vibrate, but this time, small rocks fell from the ceiling, bouncing off tables and chairs.

Then the entire ceiling started caving in.

# CHAPTER 20

"To the bunks!" Atty shouted.

I wasn't sure how that would happen since we were trapped between a giant pile of cow dung at the front door and man-eating horses at the back, but I didn't question Atty. If she said we were leaving the dining hall, then we were leaving the dining hall.

Maybe luck was on our side, because one of the walls of the dining hall collapsed. We ran for this newly formed exit and scrambled out. Atty led the way, and Jason stayed at the back, making sure we all got through okay.

"Logan, we are going to die!" Daniel shouted as columns fell down around us. He almost seemed frozen in place.

I grabbed his arm and yanked him forward. "We are not going to die. And don't you ever suggest another summer camp to your mom. Ever."

We escaped the dining hall and ran for the nearby shelter of a gazebo. Team Cerberus was already there, and the other teams were filing off in different directions, heading for their bunks. No sooner had the last group left, the entire dining hall collapsed. A huge cloud of dust puffed up in the air from all the stone falling to the ground. The smell of cow dung got stronger, if that was even possible.

Hercules leapt onto the mass of ruins and let out a battle cry. He flexed every muscle in his body and raised his head up to the sky and shouted. Maybe he was cursing Hera. Maybe he was challenging her. I didn't want to stick around to find out.

We ran for our bunk, past Mount Olympus and Lucky Rock. Atty stopped long enough to grab the Camp Hercules flag from the flagpole, and then we ran the rest of the way, through the woods, until we reached our bunk.

Atty immediately tied the flag to a tree out front, then motioned for the rest of us to join her.

"The flag will give us protection," she said.

Whether I believed that it was really possible for the flag to give us extra protection or not, I was going to take any extra help I could get. And even though there were all sorts of noises off in the distance, nothing was coming near our bunk.

I looked to the top of the bunk where the words TEAM HYDRA were carved. For a weird, awkward, moment, I was overwhelmed by happiness and pride that I was part of this team.

"Team Hydra," I said. "Best team in the world. Am I

right?"

I put up my hand to fist-bump Jason.

He immediately fist-bumped me back. "Straight up. No better team ever."

I guess everyone was feeling the love, even Atty, because then we brought it in and did one of those things where we all shouted 'Team Hydra' at the same time and threw our hands into the air.

Fine. It was way cooler than football camp would have been, monsters and everything.

Inside, we circled around in the great room.

"We get some armor," Atty said. "And we attack the Hydra . . . as a group." At this last part she looked right at me.

"Daniel and Harper were part of it, too," I said.

"I hold you to blame," Atty said.

That was just perfect.

Jason grabbed a couple pieces of wood from a bucket next to the fireplace. "We'll need a torch to fight the Hydra."

"So no new heads will grow back, right?" Daniel said. Now that we were inside and nothing was attacking us, his bravery seemed to have returned.

"Exactly," Jason said. "We cut a head off, then burn the stump."

"Except the mortal head," Daniel said. "That'll kill it."

"True," Atty said. "But with this mess that Hercules has gotten us in to, it's bound to regenerate."

I guess since Hercules wasn't around, she was okay talking a little trash about him. Of course she was right. Hercules and his curse and the broken amphora were huge problems that he was totally responsible for.

"We should have time before that happens," Jason said. "The monsters need time to build up strength and respawn. We'll have at least a week. Maybe a month. Now you each have five minutes to prepare. Get what you need and meet outside."

Since we already had our swords and spears (Camp Rules Numbers Four and Five: Carry them with you everywhere), we didn't need more weapons. But I did grab a pretty sweet shield from one of the weapons storage rooms. It would be nice to have something to block the Hydra in case she tried again to eat me for lunch. Or he.

I turned to Daniel. "Is the Hydra a boy monster or a girl monster?"

He shrugged. "Probably a girl. Most monsters are girls."

I glanced around, making sure Harper hadn't been listening. Thankfully, there was no sign of her.

Once I made sure the shield wasn't going to snap in half

at the first impact, I came out of the storage room and turned down the hallway that led back to the great room, but something really shiny caught my eye.

No, that wasn't right. I *felt* something, off to my left. Like the force of it made me actually turn my head to look. There was an open door, and through the door was a stone shelf attached to the wall. Sitting on the shelf were three apples. Three shiny golden apples, just like the one Atty had been eating on story night.

They sparkled and lit up the room around them. I was four steps forward and through the door before I even realized that I'd moved. And almost like it wasn't part of me, my arm started to lift from my side, to reach for one of the apples, because seriously, Atty had three of them. She wouldn't miss one. And I was sure the apple would come in useful for something.

I took another step. Then another. The apples were so close, I could almost taste them. Not only did they look irresistible, I knew they would taste amazing. I felt the juice dripping down my chin.

My hand was at shelf level now. My fingers touched the stone.

From outside the window, an owl hooted, shaking me from the moment. I took a step back as the spell dissolved around me. What in the world was that? Another step back. And then I couldn't get out of the room fast enough. If Atty came in here and found me, she would pull my fingernails out, no questions asked. What had I seriously been thinking? I couldn't steal one of her apples.

I was back in the hallway, but the apples taunted me. I glanced over my shoulder, one more time, to get a final look at them. The apple in the middle sparkled, like the flash of a camera had landed on it.

*You'll need me soon,* it seemed to say.

Except that was ridiculous. Apples did not talk. Even if every bit of this mythology stuff was real, apples still didn't talk. Not now. Not ever.

I turned and ran down the hallway, putting as much distance between myself and the apples as possible. I could never walk down that hallway again, that's all there was to it. I could not risk stealing one of the apples.

I rounded the corner and ran into Harper, literally.

"What'd ya find?" she asked. She'd opted against a shield, but had a metal circle thing, like a giant ring. The edge of it looked like it would slice off a finger if she wasn't careful.

I held up the shield. "This. Sweet, right?"

Harper ran her hand over the designs painted on the front. "Pretty nice. I got a chakram." She held up the circle thing.

I went to take it from her, but she pulled it back. "Don't mess with it. You'll hurt yourself if you don't know how to use it."

"And you know how to use it?"

She flicked it with her wrist and it whizzed through the air, sinking into the stone wall. Then she glared at me.

I put up my hands. "Fine. I won't use it."

She walked to the wall and yanked it free. "Where's Daniel?"

I turned back. "He was right behind me. I left him in the weapons room."

"I'm right here," Daniel said, hurrying toward us from the great room. "And you guys are late. Jason and Atty are waiting."

I had no clue how he'd gotten around me, unless he'd done it when I was looking at the apples.

We followed him back to the great room. Everyone else in our bunk stood by the door.

Atty whipped around. "It's about time, Logan."

I smiled and waved. "Sorry about that. I'm here now. We can get started."

"We already got started," Atty said. "Without you."

"What's going on?" Harper asked, clipping the circle weapon thing to a hook on her belt.

"The Hydra," Harper's roommate Mia said. "We spotted it."

 **CHAPTER 21**

**J**ason stepped forward and placed the map on the table. "I went out scouting." He pointed to a spot deep in the trees, off near the fence. "I spotted the Hydra near here, on the other side of base camp. There's a cave."

I groaned before I could stop myself. But a cave? We'd already gone into a dark cave when we visited the Underworld. Not only had there been dead things floating in the water, the entire place smelled like bat poop.

"Something you'd like to share, Logan?" Atty said.

I shook my head. I didn't want to relive the Underworld in any way, shape, or form.

"Then keep your complaints to yourself," Atty said. She stabbed a knife into the table to drive her point home.

Jason went on. "We split into three teams of four. We'll spread out and each approach it from a different side. It won't have a chance of escape."

Daniel, Harper, and I teamed up with Mia. She was taller than any kid in our bunk and so skinny that she looked like she'd been stretched, but I'd also seen her run in this race last week and knew she was probably the fastest kid in camp. We all double checked each other's weapons and then headed out.

Jason led the way, but before we left the bunk, he dipped a piece of firewood into the fire and lit it, making a torch.

"I'll be ready to move in with the fire when we get to the Hydra," Jason said.

We split up almost immediately because Jason and Atty claimed it was safest if we all took different routes. Safe was not a word I used in the same sentence as anything about Camp Hercules. The four of us had to duck to evade giant birds that tried to peck at us as we ran in and out of the woods. They almost got Daniel a couple times, but Mia grabbed his arm and dragged him faster than he could run. Then we were back inside the woods and away from the birds.

"And those were . . . ?" I asked.

Daniel opened his mouth to answer, but before he could, Mia said, "Stymphalian Birds. Their feathers are made of metal and their poop is poisonous."

I looked to Daniel whose eyes went really wide, like he couldn't believe someone else knew this. If we hadn't been at a mythology themed summer camp, I wouldn't have believed it either. But I'd come to realize that lots of people loved this mythology stuff, Daniel—and apparently Mia—included.

"They aren't after us," Mia said. "They're after the bunk trying to fight them: Team Bird."

"That's good," Harper said. "I wouldn't want to fight those."

I wasn't so sure. The Hydra wasn't much better. Right now, I was pretty jealous of the kids who were out apple picking as their labor. Like how hard could that be?

We turned to keep going when an owl hooted three times, super loudly. Someone stepped out into the path.

She was tall—taller than even Hercules—and she was wearing golden battle armor, like she was ready to go fight at the front line of a war. Her brown hair was braided and hung over her right shoulder, and on her left shoulder sat an owl. It was probably the same owl I'd been hearing.

"You won't be able to defeat the Hydra yet," she said.

Daniel's mouth fell open, and I swear he was about to fall over in shock.

"Athena?" he said.

The woman cocked her head. "Maybe."

"Oh my gosh, you are Athena," Mia said. "You are totally my favorite goddess. You could kick anyone's butt, even Ares."

I wanted to jump into the conversation, because even I'd heard of Athena. She was the goddess of . . .

"Wait," I said. "What are you the goddess of again?"

I swear Athena rolled her eyes, and she seemed to tell me that I should know this. And I knew I should know it. I just didn't know how or why I should know it.

"War," Daniel said.

"And wisdom," Mia said.

War and wisdom. That's right. I knew it now that they

said it. I must've heard it from someone at some point.

I kept looking at the owl. There was something so familiar about it. About this woman, actually. I was sure I'd seen her before, but I couldn't put my finger on where.

Then Athena held out a branch.

"Logan, take this," she said.

I didn't question her. I took the branch. It was so smooth that it was almost oily. And it wasn't very big. More like a heavy stick that fit into my fist.

"What's it for?" I asked.

"Fire," Athena said. "It's the only way to fight the Hydra."

"But Jason already has fire," Harper said. It almost felt like she was challenging Athena. But who in their right mind would do that?

Athena shook her head and the owl hooted. "Not the right kind of fire. The Hydra has gotten stronger since being in the amphora. Normal fire won't work. You four need to get immortal fire on an olive branch. It's the only way you'll be able to defeat the Hydra."

"Okay," Daniel said.

What? Was he just going to believe this Athena about some immortal fire because she said so?

"What's immortal fire?" I asked. Before I ran off and once again did exactly what Jason and Atty had told me not to do, I better have a pretty good reason.

Athena pointed in the direction of Mount Olympus. "It's the fire of the gods. Fire to defeat monsters. Fire that will last forever. Prometheus has it."

"Prometheus?" Harper said. "Is that guy even real?" She reached for her pocket, like she was going to take out her spy camera, but then stopped. I guess she remembered that she'd lost it in the Underworld.

Athena laughed. "Oh, he's real, which is kind of unfortunate for him. He's chained to the side of Mount Olympus. Find him. Get him to light this torch—not some other torch; no other torch will work. The immortal fire is the only fire that will work against the Hydra now. It's the only way."

"Are you sure?" Daniel asked, because I could tell by the way he kept not looking toward Mount Olympus that he really didn't want to break the rules.

"Totally sure," Athena said. "I know everything. Goddess of Wisdom and all."

She winked. Then, before any of us could say anything else, she walked away, back into the trees. The owl hooted once more, and then there was no sign of her.

I shouldered my shield because it was getting heavy on my arm, especially with the added weight of the olive branch.

"We can't go to Mount Olympus," Mia said. "Jason and Atty would never let us."

"We're not going to tell them," Harper said, looking at Mia like she was clueless.

"You're going to lie to the counselors?" Mia said. "Do you know how mad Atty will get?"

I didn't want to get on Atty's bad side any more than I already was. And Mia was right. They were going to freak out if we broke their rules. But it's not like the goddess of war and whatever would tell us to do something we weren't supposed to do. She was a goddess after all. If she said we needed to get some special fire, then I was going to get some special fire.

"You heard Athena," I said. "We need the fire. We have to go."

Mia bit her lip. "But Jason and Atty will notice we're gone. We can't break camp rules."

"She's right. They will notice if we're not there," Daniel said. "We can't just not show up."

They were right. But we also needed the fire.

"You two go back to the Hydra," I said. "Harper and I can check out this Promo guy."

"No way," Daniel said, glaring at me as if he couldn't believe I would leave him behind. "You're not going without me. You need me. I'm your mythology guru."

"Fine," I said. "Harper—"

"Don't even say it. You're not going without me either."

"Mia . . . ," I said.

Mia pushed her nose up in the air and crossed her arms. "I don't plan to break the rules. I'll circle around Mount Olympus and go cover our position."

Sweet! This plan was going to work out after all.

"You're the best," I said.

She scowled. "Yeah, well, if they flat out ask me where you guys are, I'm not going to lie. I'm not going to get in trouble for you."

The owl hooted three times, and Mia glanced over toward the sound. It was like Athena was watching us.

"Fine," Mia said. "Maybe I'll fib just a little. But I'm not going to be happy about it."

I hoped she wouldn't have to lie. Maybe getting the fire would be really easy.

Okay, who was I kidding? Nothing so far had been easy at camp. Nothing. There was no reason to expect this to be any different.

# CHAPTER 22

We all four dashed out of the trees. The stupid birds that we'd seen earlier immediately flew at us.

"Where is Team Bird?" I shouted as I ran from statue to column to gazebo trying to evade the things. "Shouldn't they be taking care of these things?"

Daniel ran up beside me, ducking under the arm of the statue I was hiding behind. "It's not easy to fight a Stymphalian Bird," he said. "You need—"

I put up my hand to stop him. "Unless we need to do it, I don't want to know." My mind was already so cluttered with all this mythology stuff, I wasn't sure much more would fit. I had to focus on what was important: the Hydra.

We ran for the next cover, a gazebo near the center of camp. One of the birds flew right above. Something loud thumped on the roof.

"It's the poop!" Mia shouted, and she pulled her bandana over her mouth.

A gagging smell reached my nostrils, and I couldn't get the bandana on fast enough. Once everyone was ready, we made another run for it, this time all the way to the fire pit near base camp.

I kicked Lucky Rock. "So much for being lucky. Why did we have to touch this stupid rock anyway?"

Daniel reached down and touched it. "It's for protection. And you better touch it."

I crossed my arms. "I'm not touching it. Nothing has been lucky so far. This entire camp is unlucky."

Harper pushed past me and touched the rock. "We're still alive, aren't we?"

"Barely," I said.

Mia stepped forward and touched it also.

Daniel fixed his eyes on me. "Logan, you promised me that you would touch the rock every day."

Man, I hated promises. Why did I ever make them?

"That was before this entire camp went crazy," I said. I whipped around to face Harper. "And if we hadn't stolen that dumb amphora, none of this would have happened."

Mia gasped. "You guys stole the amphora?"

I pointed to Harper. "She did. To spy for her mom."

Harper shrugged like she could not have cared less. "And obviously it was justified. I mean come on. Hercules had all the labors stored in the amphora? And he thought that was a good idea?"

"It was a good idea as long as the amphora didn't get broken," Daniel said.

"But it did," I said. "Which makes the entire thing a bad idea."

"But you guys—" Mia started.

The thunder of a hundred hooves coming our way stopped her complaining.

"Something's coming!" I shouted. "Run for Mount Olympus!"

No one argued, not even Daniel.

We ran as fast as we could. Mia got there first since she was the fastest. And no sooner were we on the slopes of the mountain of the gods, the flesh eating horses ran straight for us. There was nowhere for us to go.

Mia fell on her butt and covered her head. I tried not to, but they were getting closer every second. And then they were only ten feet away. Dust billowed in the air around them. Around us.

Then they stopped.

They stood at the base of Mount Olympus. I dared to peek out from behind my hands. The entire group of horses stared at us with red eyes, hooves pawing at the ground. Their teeth chomped like they were ready to have us as their morning snack. But they didn't come any closer.

I stood and brushed off my legs. "I don't think they can come on the mountain."

Daniel scooted back. "How can you be sure?"

"I can't," I said. "But look at them. Poor little horses can't come any farther."

Harper smacked my arm. "Don't taunt them."

Yeah, maybe it wasn't a good idea to make fun of mythological creatures that could eat you.

"Okay, I'm leaving now," Mia said.

"Wait! You aren't gonna say anything about the amphora, are you?" I asked.

Mia glanced at Harper and then back at me. Maybe they had some kind of roommate bond going on, because Mia said, "No, I'm not going to say anything. But just please hurry. I don't like this whole thing at all."

It wasn't like any of us liked it. And if there was some other way, like a magical word I could say to control all the labors, I would have done it in a second. But there wasn't.

"We'll hurry," Daniel said. And he smiled really big at her.

Mia ran off, and we dashed up the side of Mount Olympus. The crazy killer horses stayed there for a good half hour. I know because I kept turning around to check. Finally, they shifted around, all at once, and ran back in the direction of the bunks. Team Horse better deal with these guys before they ate someone.

"Where do we find this Promo guy?" I said.

"Pro-me-the-us," Daniel said, sounding out every syllable.

"Whatever," I said. "This mountain is pretty big. How are we supposed to find some guy chained to the side of it?"

Daniel held his arms apart really wide. "First, it's not just some guy, Logan. It's Prometheus."

"Right." I waited for him to explain why that mattered.

"He's a Titan," Daniel said. "That means he's really big."

"So he's big," Harper said. "This is still a pretty big mountain."

I looked up the mountain. The top wasn't even visible through the clouds. We'd climbed part way up before when we'd stolen the amphora from Hercules.

"True," Daniel said. "But finding him is easy. All we have to do is look for the eagle."

"Another big bird?" I said. "Seriously? What is up with these big birds? First we had that harpy thing that was guarding the amphora, then—"

"Wait," Daniel said. "Maybe we can get my lucky quarter back from the harpy while we're here."

"We're not getting your quarter back," I said. "I don't want to see a harpy ever again. But what about the eagle? What does it do?"

Daniel shook his head. "You don't want to know."

Given everything else, that was probably true.

"Guys," Harper said. "I see some big birds." She pointed way up high. Two birds flew around in a circle, dipping in and out of the clouds.

"That's got to be it!" Daniel said, and he took off climbing way faster than we had been. I guess the promise of seeing more of these weird mythology things was enough to make him forget about how he didn't want to break the rules.

We hurried after him, circling around Mount Olympus until we were nearly on the other side. The closer we got, the better view we had of the birds. They had huge white heads that blended into the sky and dark bodies, and their beaks were hooked like something out of a pirate story.

"I think I see him," Daniel shouted.

Harper and I hurried to join him. And there, chained to a rock on the side of Mount Olympus was the biggest person I'd ever seen in my life.

I was about to open my mouth and make some sarcastic comment about how someone that big should be able to break the wimpy little chains that were holding him, but then one of the eagles dove straight for us.

# CHAPTER 23

The closer the eagle got, the more I was able to see that it was super-sized, just like the guy chained to the mountain. It could have swallowed my arm in one gulp. Actually, it was about to. I held my shield in front of me. The eagle screeched almost like the shield scared it. Then it changed course and dove for the man on the mountain.

"What is it doing?" I whispered, hoping the eagle didn't change its mind and come back our way.

"It's eating his liver," Daniel said.

"His what?"

"His liver," Daniel said. "That's what the eagle does."

I peeked out from behind the shield. Sure enough, that's what it looked like the eagle was doing.

"Why in the world would an eagle eat this Promo guy's liver?" That was weirdest thing I'd ever heard. Mom made liver one time at home. She claimed it was some kind of delicacy, and she made a big deal of it and even got sparkling grape juice to go along with it, like it was a fancy meal.

One word: disgusting.

Liver was about the worst thing I'd ever tasted. I'd run upstairs and brushed my teeth five times and still hadn't been able to get the taste out of my mouth.

"Wait! I remember this story," Harper said. "Prometheus gave humans fire, and Zeus got mad. So he had Prometheus chained to a mountain and made an eagle eat his liver."

"That's nasty," I said.

Harper gritted her teeth. "And the worst part is that it happens every day. Each night the liver grows back so the next day the eagle can eat it again."

I looked to Daniel for confirmation. He nodded.

I shuddered. "That has to hurt."

The eagle lifted into the air and flew to the top of a column, where it perched along with the other eagle. I wasn't too excited to run over there yet.

"That was his punishment," Daniel said.

"And we're asking him for fire? He's not going to give it to us. Why would he?"

"We don't have much choice," Harper said.

She had a good point. Our options were pretty limited. The labors were going to destroy camp if we failed.

We gave it a good five minutes. I tried everything I could to be patient, but each minute we wasted, all I could imagine was the Hydra eating all the kids in our bunk for lunch. After as long as I could wait, I ducked out from the rock we were hiding behind and started over for the Promo guy.

The eagles swooped down, like they wanted to check me out. I held the shield in front of my stomach. No way was I letting them eat my liver.

"Hey, what's up?" I said to the Titan, trying to sound super casual. I didn't want to freak him out before we'd even had the chance to ask him for immortal fire.

Prometheus slowly turned his giant head to look in our direction. He had to be at least thirty feet tall.

Daniel elbowed me. "You don't talk to a god that way."

"Like you have a lot of experience talking to gods," I said. "How would you know how to talk to gods?"

"I just know," Daniel said.

"He's right," Harper said. "You have to show gods respect."

She pushed ahead of both of us and got directly in his line of sight. "Hi, we're campers here at Camp Hercules, and it is such an honor to meet you. I used to read stories about you when I was little. Of all the Titans, I loved your story the most."

Harper had read stories about Titans as a little kid? What kind of parents did she have anyway?

"Go away," Prometheus said, and looked back upward . . . right at the eagles.

"Did you name them?" I asked.

Daniel elbowed me again, but I ignored him.

"Itchy and Scratchy," Prometheus said. "They take turns."

I suppressed a shudder, but the image of the eagles eating

his liver, like actually eating it, was still so fresh in my mind.

"Those are great names! Which one is worse?"

Harper put her hand on her forehead and shook her head, like she couldn't believe I was actually asking.

"Scratchy," Prometheus said. He didn't hesitate even a single second.

I jumped up on a rock so I could see his middle section. His clothes were all torn everywhere, leaving only scraps to cover the essentials, but his stomach was completely visible. Whatever the eagle had done to him was healing over right in front of my eyes.

"So it really heals?" I said.

"Too fast," he said. "The healing hurts worse than the eagles."

"Really?"

Prometheus nodded and yanked on the chains that held his arms over his head. "I can't scratch anything. It drives me nuts. And it's not even where they attack. It's everywhere. Do you know how horrible it is when you have an itch and you can't reach it?"

"Oh, I know," Daniel said. "I broke my arm when I was little and had to wear a cast."

A fresh wave of guilt rolled over me.

"Yeah, well that's my life. It sucks."

Great. This was not the way I'd hoped the conversation would go. Depressing him wasn't going to make him want to give us fire.

"Why did you do it?" Harper asked, cutting in before I could ask anything else. "You knew you'd get in trouble. You knew Zeus would be furious. But you still did it. Why?"

She had a gift for stringing out one question after another.

"Because people needed fire," Prometheus said. "I created people, but they had to have fire to live. If I didn't give it to them, they would have died."

That was good. I could totally play off this need thing.

"Do you know who we are?" I asked, jumping down from the rock.

Prometheus turned his head so he could take a long look at us. I tried to look as worthy as I could, whatever that meant. But then he turned away, back to the sky where Itchy and Scratchy sat on the top of the column.

"No idea," he said.

"We're here for Camp Hercules," Daniel said, and he went on to give the entire explanation of what Camp Hercules was and how we were sorted into bunks and that our T-shirts and bandanas protected us and how Hercules had stored the labors inside the amphora and then it had broken. Prometheus kept letting out little noises, like he had a bone stuck in his throat. The last thing we needed was for him to choke and die. By the time Daniel had finished talking, tears leaked out of the corners of Prometheus' eyes.

He was laughing.

At us.

"Great Zeus, that is good," Prometheus said. "Hercules has gotten into good trouble this time."

"Yeah, funny, right?" I said. "But we need your help."

At this, the laughs stopped.

"My help?"

We all three nodded. "We need immortal fire," Harper said. She held out the stick that Athena had given us. "We need you to light this so we can use it to fight the Hydra. Without it, I don't think we can defeat the monster."

This made Prometheus start laughing again. "Oh that's perfect. The Hydra is even stronger, and only my fire can stop new heads from growing."

I tried to look as pathetic as I possibly could. "So will you help us?"

Prometheus flipped his hand around as much as was possible with the chains. A ball of fire burst to life on his palm. Relief flowed through me. This was going to work.

"Sure, I'll help you," Prometheus said.

"Than—" Daniel started.

"If . . . ," Prometheus said. He clenched his hand into a fist, and the fire went out.

"If what?"

"If you free me."

# CHAPTER 24

Free Prometheus? Fine. We could handle that.

I walked up to where his giant wrist was chained to the rocks of Mount Olympus. It took a lot of steps since he was a Titan and was really tall. The chain was attached to a hook that was driven into the rock. I grabbed hold of the chain and started pulling.

It didn't budge.

"Hey, kid?" Prometheus said. "If I could have just given it a tug, don't you think I'd be free by now?"

He had a point.

I pulled my sword from the hook on my belt and swung it down, chopping at the connection. Atty herself had approved my sword, and it was pretty awesome. It had to work.

"Mortal weapons won't cut through the chain," Prometheus said. "Duh."

Okay, this Titan had a serious attitude. I was doing the best that I could.

"Fine," I said. "How do you suggest we free you? Because I'm fine with doing it. I just need to know how."

But Daniel was shaking his head so fiercely, I though his neck would get whiplash.

"We can't free him, Logan," Daniel said.

"Of course we can. We need immortal fire. He has it. It seems a pretty fair exchange."

Daniel looked upward, toward the top of Mount Olympus. "Zeus will be mad."

"Zeus," I laughed. "Like he's even real."

Lightning shot out of the sky so fast that I jumped. My teeth hit together hard.

"Of course he's real," Daniel whispered. "Remember? It's all real."

I took a deep breath. Then another. And another. I had to keep the thought fresh in my mind. All this weird mythology stuff was real. I knew that, and yet my mind still didn't want to believe it. But if a giant guy could be chained to the side of a mountain having his liver eaten by an eagle every single day, then there could be a god living at the top of this mountain who threw lightning bolts when he got mad.

"Okay, fine, he's real," I said. "We still need the fire."

"Which means you still need to free me," Prometheus said.

Harper sauntered up next to me and put her hands on her hips. "How do we free you?"

Prometheus smiled. "You need a weapon of the gods.

Only a weapon of the gods will cut through the chains. Bring that back and free me, and I'll give you immortal fire."

"But the Hydra is destroying camp," I said.

"Camp!" The Titan laughed. "If you think camp is my biggest concern, then you have no idea who you're talking to."

Yeah, camp did seem pretty trivial when a giant bird was making a snack of your insides each day.

"Where do we get a weapon of the gods?" I asked.

Prometheus groaned, and I think it was because he thought we were all idiots.

"From the gods," he said. "It's pretty obvious."

Daniel looked right at me. "Before you suggest it, I am not stealing a weapon from Zeus. No way. So don't ask."

I had to agree. After the lightning bolt, it didn't seem like the best idea.

"Aren't there a bunch of gods?" I said. "We could ask that Athena lady. She might give us a weapon."

"I don't care who you get it from," Prometheus said. "Just get it. I've had as much of these eagles as I can handle. In fact, there is one more condition."

I almost argued with him that he couldn't go adding conditions, but I bit my tongue.

"What?" Harper said, super sweetly.

"Cover my stomach with one of those bandanas," Prometheus said. "I can't take it anymore."

"But Camp Rule—" Daniel started.

I put up my hand to stop him. This was a simple request and totally worth it. Also, it would show our good faith. And

I could get the bandana back when we returned. I untied my bandana and jumped up onto the rock. Then I placed it over his stomach.

"Now hurry," Prometheus said. "Bonus points if you get it done before tomorrow."

So much for a thank you.

Itchy and Scratchy screeched, almost like they were listening in, then they flew off their perch and started circling.

"We can do it by tomorrow," I said.

I had no idea how, but we'd figure it out.

# CHAPTER 25

We left Prometheus there, on the side of Mount Olympus with the eagles flying overhead. It would really stink to be in his position, having to suffer the exact same torture every single day. I wondered if it got a little boring after a while.

We ran down the side of Mount Olympus like the harpies were after us, even though there was nothing in sight. Lucky Rock was there at the bottom, and since everything was going in our favor, I reached out and touched it again.

"Thanks so far," I said. Sure, a lot of everything wasn't so lucky, like camp being destroyed, but we were well on the way to defeating the Hydra.

"What about the Fates?" Daniel said.

"What about them?" I asked.

"They're gods," he said. "I mean they're immortal. And I

142

bet we could buy something that will cut right through those chains."

I thought about it. "That's a really great idea. And we're pretty close. It's just on the other side of the mountain."

"Do you think we can make it?" Daniel asked.

I looked around, but there was no sign of any monsters right now. The giant pile of poop was still visible in front of the collapsed rubble of the dining hall, but all the actual creatures were gone.

"We can totally make it. And now's the perfect time."

"I'll catch up with you guys," Harper said.

We both turned to look at her. "Why? Where are you going?"

She shook her head. "There's something I need to check."

"What?"

"I don't want to tell you yet, in case I'm wrong."

"Wrong about what?" I asked.

"I'll tell you later," Harper said. "Just go to the Trading Post and meet back here."

"But—" I started.

She put up her hand. "Don't say a word about me going off alone. I'm fine. Just hurry up."

Without another word, she set off toward the front of camp. I looked to Daniel, who shrugged. Then we crept in the direction of the Trading Post.

It was closed. At least that's what the sign out front said. It was like all the other signs around camp—a statue of a lady with a blindfold holding her hand up and from her hand was a sign on a chain with funny letters and an eyeball.

# CLOSED

## ENTRY WITHOUT PERMISSION WILL COST 50 YEARS.

"That's just perfect," Daniel said. "This would have been the easiest way."

"I don't know about that," I said. "It might have cost you five years off your life to buy something from them."

"My life!" Daniel said. "Why would it have been off my life?"

I'd already lost fifteen minutes with the whole Cerberus thing.

"Because you've given them less time than I have so far. Remember Cerberus?"

"Cerberus was your idea, not mine," Daniel said. "Maybe we could have split it."

I rattled the doorknob, but it was locked. "Well, it doesn't matter now. They aren't here."

We turned to leave, and there they were in their black leather pants and colored tank tops.

"What are you doing, Sugar Plum?" the Fate on the left in red said. She held the iPad of Doom.

"We . . . need . . . ," Daniel started.

Seeing them here, I wasn't sure I really wanted to do business with them at all. I almost felt the minutes slipping away.

"We need a weapon of the gods," I said. "You know, something that the gods might use."

All three stared at me. But it wasn't like they should be surprised. I had the feeling that the Fates knew everything before it ever happened.

"A weapon of the gods?" the Fate on the right said. She held a nasty long pair of scissors which she opened and closed.

"Yeah . . . um . . . it's to . . . um . . . ," Daniel said.

"It's to fight the labors," I said. It wasn't technically a lie. We need it to get the fire to fight the labors. It was just a few steps removed.

"Oh, sorry, Dumpling. We can't help you with that," the one in the middle said. At least that was what came out of her mouth. But what it really seemed like she said was, *"You don't want to pay the price."*

"But—" I started.

All three Fates turned their heads, like they were listening to something far away. I didn't hear anything, not even their voices in my head.

"Interesting," the one in the middle said.

"What's interesting?" Daniel asked, coming up with enough courage to talk finally.

"Oh, you'll find out soon enough, Sweet Pea," the Fate on the left said. But again, their voices did that weird thing where I heard something else in my mind. I swear that she said, *"Don't trust anyone."*

My head snapped to Daniel, and he did the same, looking right at me.

"Did you hear that?" I said.

He nodded. *"Listen to the sign.* That's what they said."

I shook my head. "That's not what they said. They said—" I turned to look back at the Fates, but they were gone.

"Where'd they go?" Daniel asked. "I don't know what kind of sign to listen to."

I hadn't heard anything about a sign. I'd heard not to trust anyone. But if I wasn't supposed to trust anyone, then did that include Daniel? Maybe I shouldn't tell him what they said.

"A sign? That could be anything." I started down the steps, but stopped at the statue. "Like this sign? There are signs like this all over camp."

"I know," Daniel said. He kicked at the statue. It started to wobble, but I grabbed it to steady it.

I was about to complain some more about how mysterious the Fates were, but then I remembered the whole thing with Cerberus and the Underworld.

"I guess we just have to trust them," I said. So far, the Fates hadn't let us down.

"Trust the Fates!" Daniel said. "That would be a cool t-shirt."

"Yeah, maybe when this whole mess is over, we can make some."

We hurried back toward Lucky Rock to meet Harper, but she met us halfway.

"Did you guys get anything?" she asked.

We shook our heads and told her about the Fates.

"A sign?" she said. "What is that—"

I stopped her. "Yeah, we have no clue. But we're going to trust the Fates."

"Bad idea," Harper said. "You know you can't trust them, right?"

"Why?"

Harper stammered, like she didn't really know herself. "You just can't. That's all. Anyway, let's get back to the group before anyone notices that we're gone."

It turned out that everyone was on their way back to the Team Hydra bunk. And when I say everyone, I mean literally everyone. Every single person at camp—including campers and counselors—was pouring through the door.

We ran up the steps to where Jason and Atty stood. If they noticed we'd been missing, they didn't say anything. There was no sign of Mia. She must've already been inside.

"What's going on?" I said.

Jason was counting people off on a clipboard as they came in.

"All the other bunks got destroyed," Atty said. She pointed out front. "Only reason we didn't is because of the flag."

"It really protected us?" Daniel said. "That's awesome."

"Yeah, awesome," Atty said. "Except now everyone's staying here. And if someone messes with my apples, I'll put itching powder in their underwear."

I had no doubt that she'd do it. But man, those apples were tempting. I curled my fingers into fists.

Jason pushed us through the door. "Stay inside. The labors will only be worse at night."

That was the least comforting piece of information that we'd had yet. It was going to be a long night.

147

# CHAPTER 26

Jason and Atty slammed and locked the door as soon as everyone was inside.

"That's one-hundred-forty-four campers and twenty-four counselors," Jason said, dropping the clipboard on a table in the great room. Which was packed, by the way. They'd set up sleeping bags in all the rooms and even in the hallways. Our room, which normally only Daniel and I slept in, now had twenty kids. Nobody better snore.

"Logan and Daniel, start the fire," Jason said.

I froze. Did he know about the whole Prometheus thing? But no, he couldn't possibly. He'd been in the forest, hunting the Hydra. It was just a coincidence.

I put all my Cub Scout abilities to use and managed to get a small spark by hitting some rocks together. There was a tiny bit of smoke, but no fire.

"Here, let someone who knows what they're doing try it," Ryan, from Team Cerberus, said.

"I got it," I said, because no way was I going to let him prove he was better than me at anything. I tried the whole spark thing again.

I swear the fireplace was mocking me. The tiny bit of smoke that appeared curled up and disappeared.

Ryan grabbed a couple rocks and struck them together. A huge spark flew out and the logs burst into flames. He dropped the rocks and dusted his hands off.

"That's how you do it," he said.

"Whatever." I would have bet my sword that he bought fire-starting skills from the Fates or something. I hoped it cost him more than five minutes off his life.

He stood and towered over me. And I was not short. He was just really tall. "You know you shouldn't have messed with Cerberus. You should have let us catch him and return him to the Underworld."

I stood also, trying to make myself as tall as possible. I was only maybe an inch or so shorter. "You guys weren't having much luck. Somebody had to clean up the mess you made."

"Yeah, well, now we have to go back to the Underworld and get him again. And that's your fault."

The way I figured, nothing was my fault. This entire mess was all Hercules' fault for putting the labors in the amphora in the first place. Or maybe it was Hera's fault for cursing him to do the labors over and over again.

"Have fun in the Underworld," I said, and shouldered

past Ryan.

We barred the doors and windows and sat around the campfire pretending we didn't hear the monsters outside while we listened to all the counselors tell stories. And the thing was that every single story was epic. Like amazing and scary things happened. Achilles told some story about a war that lasted for ten years and a horse they had to hide inside.

"It's called the Trojan Horse," Daniel whispered to me and Harper. "They hid inside and made the Trojans think it was a present."

"That's pretty smart," I said.

"It won them the war," Harper said.

Achilles stopped talking and looked at us. "Would you three like to tell the story?"

We shook our heads, and he finished the story. His side won.

"But you're forgetting the rest of the story," one of the other counselors said. It was an older guy, maybe even thirty, who wore a giant bow over his shoulder at all times.

"That's Odysseus," Daniel said.

"O-D-C-Us?" I said, sounding it out. I doubted it was spelled how it sounded.

Daniel nodded but didn't say another word, and the Odysseus guy told this crazy awesome story about how it took him ten years to sail home from that war because some god that lived in the water named Poseidon got really mad at him. There were whirlpools that came alive and tried to drown the guys on the boats, there were sirens that sang beautiful music to get the men to jump to their deaths, and there were cannibals that ate the men.

"Why are there no women in the story?" Harper asked, loud enough for everyone to hear.

A bunch of other girls in the group nodded, like they were wondering the same thing.

"Would you really want there to be girls in the story?" I said. "Everyone died."

Odysseus looked really sad when I said this last part, but then he smiled and said, "Women on ships is bad luck."

"Bad luck!" Harper said. "Maybe if you'd had some women on board, none of those bad things would have happened."

She had a good point. From the story he was telling, they'd had about the worst luck I'd ever heard of in my life. Maybe he should have bartered with the Fates for a safer journey. Or maybe there were some things the Fates couldn't control.

Cassie, one of the girl counselors, was about to tell a story next, but just then, a loud knock sounded out.

Jason and Atty were immediately on their feet. They braced against the door just as another knock came.

"Let me in!" Hercules shouted from outside.

I've never seen the counselors move so fast. They lifted the bar and unbolted the door. Hercules dashed inside. Unfortunately, so did one of the giant Stymphalian Birds.

# CHAPTER 27

The bird was red and black and looked like it was made of leather and covered with metal feathers. It flew in through the door before Jason and Atty could slam it shut. Hercules leapt forward, trying to catch the bird, but it dipped up and down before he got a hand on it.

"Counselors! Get ready!" Hercules shouted.

Every single counselor was on their feet, favorite weapon in their hand. They stabbed at the bird as it flew around the room, knocking over vases and pedestals and statues. It flew at the fire and threw logs all around the room, like it was trying to catch the whole place on fire. And then it pooped.

"Bandanas on!" Atty shouted.

I did not need to be told twice. The stench was horrifyingly overwhelming. I grabbed for my bandana and realized that I didn't have it. The stench got stronger.

I elbowed Daniel. "Let me share."

He immediately untied it so we could both hold his bandana over our mouths.

Everyone got so distracted by the poisonous poop that the bird managed to sink its claws into Will, the kid from Team Cow Stable who'd broken the amphora. It lifted him high up into the air and flew to a corner. Metal feathers pulled away from its leathery skin and flew at us. They stuck in the walls and floor like spikes.

"William, stay strong!" Hercules shouted, and he vaulted up into the air, like he was going to grab the kid and destroy the bird all at the same time.

The bird had other ideas. It dipped away from Hercules and flew behind a line of ten statues sitting on a high shelf near the ceiling.

Will looked like he was ready to pee his pants. The claws of the bird sank into his shoulders, and even with the protection of the camp shirts, it had to hurt.

Then Odysseus unslung his giant bow and put an arrow on it. He pulled back, and I swear the muscles in his arms looked like they would pop from under his dark skin. Then he let go.

The arrow flew through the air, passing each statue by less than an inch until it finally hit the bird. The bird flew backward and stuck to the wall, but not before it dropped Will. He fell to the ground and landed on four other kids, flattening them. They all groaned.

"How many of those birds are there?" I asked. Just one was bad. I couldn't imagine an entire flock of them.

"At least a hundred," Daniel said.

Thankfully there was only one Hydra. Sure, it had ten heads, but once we got the immortal fire, we'd take care of those no problem.

Hercules and the counselors made us all go back to the rooms while they talked.

"Let's listen in," Harper said, pulling us aside while everyone pushed and shoved to get away from the poisonous bird poop that still piled in clumps around the great room. We ducked into the kitchen and waited for everyone to leave.

"You let a bird into our bunk," Atty said to Hercules.

Jason elbowed her. "You think he didn't notice?"

"Just pointing it out," Atty said.

Hercules stood tall and lifted his arms, like he was stretching out his muscles. "It's been following me all day. I took care of ten already. But more keep coming. They're much stronger than before."

It was like Athena had said about the Hydra. All the

monsters had probably gotten stronger.

Atty scowled. "Because of the amphora."

Hercules rocked his head from one side to the other as he stretched out his neck, and then he jogged in place a little. "Yes, because of the amphora. And without the amphora, we have no control of them. The only hope we have is to defeat them and buy time before they regenerate."

"There are a lot of Stymphalian Birds," Odysseus said. He was head of Team Bird so he would know. "We defeated a couple today, but it almost destroyed us."

Helen, Achilles' co-counselor, blew out a long breath. "That's going to be really bad if the outside world finds out. Can you imagine this on the news? We'd have cameras lined up outside the gates."

At the world *news*, Harper reached for her pocket, like she wanted her camera pen.

"Which is why we can't open the gates or let the outside world find out," Hercules said. "We need to resolve this."

Achilles leaned his shield against a wall and sat in the circle with the rest of the counselors. "How? From what I've seen of most of these teams, they aren't going to be able to complete the labors if the monsters are really stronger."

I almost said something to defend our team right there and then. Team Hydra was totally capable of taking out the Hydra, especially once we got the fire. Just because Achilles' team had captured Cerberus before anyone else was done with their labors didn't mean anything. But a smart little voice inside my head told me to keep my mouth shut.

"I have a solution," Hercules said. He stood in the center

of the group and went through a series of poses, like he was in the Mister Universe contest.

"Great," Jason said. "What's the solution?"

Hercules shifted from flexing his biceps to his quads. The guy had so many muscles, just flexing them each alone would take all day. "I am going to get a new amphora."

"That could work," Harper whispered. "I wonder where he got the first one."

"But that means—" Jason started.

"Yes," Hercules said. "That means I need to visit Hephaestus."

Daniel mouthed Hephaestus, like it was a really big deal. I had no idea what it was.

"But Hephaestus hates you," Achilles said. "He'll never give you another one. Especially not since you broke the first one."

Oh, so Hephaestus was a person. Or maybe a god. Yeah, a god. That made more sense.

Hercules started doing squats, right there in the middle of the great room. "I have to try. It's the only way to capture the labors again. Because if we don't capture them, and if for some reason they get out of camp, the entire world will be at risk. We can't let that happen, people. No matter what."

"When are you going?" Jason said.

Hercules interlaced his fingers and cracked all his knuckles at once. "Now."

Atty tilted her head and looked at him like he was crazy. "But you've been out there fighting all day. You should rest."

Hercules placed a hand on her shoulder. "Atalanta, I'll

rest later. For now, this is my responsibility." He put on his best serious look, like he was ready to save the world.

Atty nodded. "Okay, I'll come with you. Hephaestus and I have that blacksmith bond. He may listen to me."

Maybe it was a pride thing, but Hercules shook his head. "I need to do this alone. You all have responsibilities here. You need to protect the campers."

Protect! If someone wanted to protect the campers, they never would have come up with this whole Camp Hercules idea in the first place. But the time to think about that was gone.

"Are you sure?" Jason said. "You should bring at least one of us."

"It's too dangerous," Hercules said. "You know Hephaestus."

If this god Hephaestus was worse than fighting poisonous birds and the Hydra, then he must be pretty horrible.

"Still . . . ," Jason said.

"No, it's decided," Hercules said. "I go alone."

"What's Hephaestus?" I whispered. "Is it a god?"

Daniel nodded. "He's the god of volcanos and metalworking. He makes all sorts of cool stuff for the gods. Like shields and swords and chains and apples and—"

"Like Atty's apples," I said.

"Yeah, exactly," Daniel said. "He made those."

"And he must've made the original amphora for Hercules," Harper said. "All the stuff he makes has special powers."

At the words special powers, my brain perked up. Chains. Weapons. Wait a second. This was exactly what we needed.

"You think he makes knives and stuff?" I asked.

"Of course," Daniel said. "Anything in the world the gods need, he makes it."

"That's perfect," I said.

Daniel's face froze. "What do you mean?"

"I mean that we need a godly weapon," I said. "So we're going to visit Hephaestus also."

# CHAPTER 28

"We can't leave the bunk," Daniel said. "Jason and Atty will never let us."

Harper was completely on board, though. "It's not like we're going to ask their permission."

Daniel's mouth dropped open. "We can't sneak out. There are monsters out there."

I'd known Daniel way longer than her. I knew how his mind worked.

"Daniel, we have to do this. Our entire bunk is counting on us. They may not know it, but they are. If we don't get the fire, then the Hydra could eat someone. And you do not want to see one of your fellow bunkmates get eaten by the Hydra and know that you could have done something to stop it, do you?"

I crossed my arms and waited. It was an amazing speech.

Flawless. Daniel kept opening and closing his mouth, like he was trying to think of some reason to say no. Finally he nodded.

"Fine," he whispered. "But how are we going to get out? All the doors are locked."

Harper rolled her eyes. "Like that matters."

I tried to figure out where she was going with the comment, but had no idea. "Doesn't it?"

"No, Logan. It doesn't matter. I can unlock anything."

Add lock-picking to the list of secret skills Harper had. She was full of surprises.

We hid in the pantry because Hercules came into the kitchen. I swear he ate everything in sight. Just watching him eat made my stomach hurt. But finally, after three sandwiches, twelve cookies, and a gallon of whole milk, he told the counselors he was leaving.

"Don't open the door for anyone," he said, as they lifted the bar holding the door shut.

"Last chance," Atty said to him. "I won't offer again."

Hercules put his hands on his hips and stood tall. "I go alone."

He had more drama than Daniel's older sister. And she was in eighth grade. We watched him leave. Jason and Atty put the bar back in place. Immediately, from outside, the birds of doom began to scream.

"Let's go," Harper said.

She led us to the girls' side of the bunk, down to the very end of the hallway, and into a bathroom.

"Hey, why is your bathroom so much nicer than ours?"

I said. It's not that the boys' bathroom was bad. It's just that the girls had two sofas, a bookcase filled with books, and a . . .

"Is that a piano?" Daniel said. He lifted the cover like he was going to start playing Beethoven right there.

"Don't touch anything." Harper walked through the piano part of the bathroom and into a separate room. At the end of the room was a door, sealed shut like all the others.

"What's this room for?" I asked. It was empty except for a mirror on the wall.

"I don't know," Harper said. "Maybe to practice fighting."

"You guys practice fighting in front of a mirror?"

"No," Harper said. "But I don't know what else it would be for."

The mirror almost seemed to flicker as we walked past, but I'm sure that was my imagination.

I pulled on the door, but it didn't budge.

"It's locked," Harper said, and then she pulled some sort of long things that looked like five different sized safety pins hooked together on a loop from her pocket and started messing with it. In under ten seconds, it popped open.

She slid the safety pins back into her pocket. "We'll leave it unlocked and come back this way."

"And you're sure this is a good idea?" Daniel said, looking back one last time. Nothing was there except the mirror.

I grabbed hold of his arm and pulled him through the door. "It's the only idea."

"Yeah, but—"

"But nothing. Let's go."

Harper closed the door after we were through. The dark night immediately swallowed us, and I couldn't make out anything except maybe some trees. I turned to figure out which way was the front. That's where Hercules would be.

We didn't make a sound as we skirted around the side of the bunk. I jumped every time the wind blew. Anything could be a monster waiting to attack us. Hercules was already way far away when we finally spotted him. He wasn't heading back to base camp, toward Mount Olympus. Instead he was jogging to the right, away from the bunks.

We hurried to catch up so we didn't lose track of him.

"Where do you think he's going?" I asked. It would be nice to know just in case we lost him in the darkness.

"Well, Hephaestus lives in a volcano," Daniel said.

I stifled a laugh. "A volcano! It's not like there are volcanos around Austin."

Daniel stopped walking and fixed his eyes on me. "This is Camp Hercules, Logan. Anything is possible."

I realized how right he was as we followed Hercules through the woods and around the river. An owl hooted in the darkness, so close I turned to look over my left shoulder. I didn't see anything. But when I turned back and we came around the edge of a bunch of trees, there it was.

A smoking volcano loomed in front of us.

# CHAPTER 29

It was a little volcano, but it was still a volcano. It wasn't very tall, which would explain why I'd never noticed it above the trees. Not like Mount Olympus which you could see from anywhere at camp. Instead, this volcano was only about as tall as our house. Smoke poured from the top like our next door neighbor's grill when he made pork chops, and lava oozed out, flowing down the sides.

"I guess we're in the right place," I said.

"Yeah, but where is Hercules?" Daniel said.

There was no sign of him anywhere. But there was a sign staked into the ground. Next to the sign was a path that led around the side of the volcano.

"We don't have an appointment," Daniel whispered.

I started forward. "That's okay. We don't actually want to talk to him."

Actually, the last thing we wanted to do was to talk to this blacksmith god.

We crept down the path, around to the back of the volcano. A wooden door was set into the side of the volcano.

"It's open," Harper said, putting her locksmith safety pins back into her pocket. "That's lucky."

"That's because Hercules is here," Daniel said. "And we shouldn't be. I'm telling you guys, this is a really bad idea."

I tried not to roll my eyes. "We've been over this. We have to do this."

Daniel scuffed his foot on the gravel around the base of the volcano. "I know. But it's still not a good idea."

Lava dripped over the top of the open door, pooling on the ground below. I stepped over the pool of lava and ducked so it wouldn't drip on me and then went inside. Harper came next followed by Daniel.

"Don't say anything," I whispered, putting a finger to my mouth.

They both nodded.

Lava flowed everywhere, which was great in that it lit up the path ahead. It was also not great in that it was hot enough to sear off our skin. Some dripped on my shirt, but didn't burn the fabric.

Did I mentioned that I loved my camp T-shirt? Wearing it was a camp rule I was happy to follow.

Up ahead the light got brighter, and I heard voices. Two voices. I squatted down and kept going until we came to a split in the path. One path led upward and to the right, and the other led forward. The voices were coming from ahead, so I hurried up the other path as quietly as possible. A low rock wall ran the whole length of the path, ensuring that I wouldn't fall to my doom right in the middle of the talking gods. Then I peeked over.

There was Hercules, hands crossed in front of him so his chest muscles looked extra big. Across from him was a guy completely covered in black smoke, like he'd been in front of a campfire for two months straight.

"It's Hephaestus," Daniel said. He kept his voice really low, but there was no hiding the fact that he was so excited he might fall off the rock wall.

I nodded.

"Can you make out what they're saying?" Harper said.

I strained to hear, but it was a bunch of mumbled words.

Hercules kept flashing his big white teeth in a smile, but the smoke-covered guy growled and snarled at every word.

"No," I said. "But it doesn't matter. Let's look for something to cut the chains."

We continued up the path, and maybe the Fates were on our side, because we hit the literal jackpot. Ahead of us was a room full of every sort of treasure I could have ever imagined. There were at least twenty shields, and I wanted every single one. There were swords and spears. A bunch of suits of armor lined the walls. Helmets and crowns hung from hooks. On a table were a handful of fancy boxes. And next to those were four other amphoras just like the one that had been broken at camp.

"We should grab one of those!" Daniel said, immediately walking to the table.

I pulled him back. "They're too big to hide. And Hercules is here to get one anyway."

"What about a knife?" Harper said.

I turned to see her holding a shiny knife. The handle sparkled from the lava flowing around the sides of the room and the floor. From the looks of it, I would have sworn it was pure gold.

"That looks perfect," I said. "Grab it and let's go."

"But . . . ," Daniel said, casting a longing glance at some of the boxes.

And I couldn't blame him. Every single thing in here was amazing, like way better than the stuff the Fates were selling at the Trading Post. I walked toward one of the crowns. I really wanted it. I could almost feel it on my head.

Then the owl hooted. I wasn't sure if it was in my mind or if Harper and Daniel heard it, too. I turned, but they weren't even looking at me. And the crown was amazing. Just a thin band of gold with a single black stone embedded in it. And it was so small. No one would even notice it was gone.

I checked behind me one more time, and then I grabbed it and tucked it under my shirt.

"Logan!" Harper said. "We need to go. And Daniel's not listening."

I hurried across the room and grabbed hold of Daniel's shirt, pulling him. "We need to go. The knife is all we need."

My face burned, because all I could think about was the crown I'd taken. Something about it made me sure I needed it.

"Look at this box," Daniel said. His fingers barely brushed one of the boxes on the table. At the small touch, it started glowing.

"Now," I said, and pulled him again.

The box was trouble. I felt it deep inside me. It had to stay here.

"But I just have to see inside," Daniel said, and he lifted the lid, the smallest amount.

Light poured out.

I slammed the lid closed so quickly, I almost took off one of his fingers.

"Look at the sign," I said, pointing to a sign right by the box.

# Do Not Open
## Under Any Circumstances

Daniel shook his head, like he was trying to clear it, then his eyes returned to normal.

"I didn't see the sign," he said.

"You didn't see it, or you didn't want to see it?" I said.

He looked really guilty, like he'd just eaten cookies before dinner.

"The Fates told you to listen to the sign, and you ignored them," I said. "This had to be the sign they were talking about."

"It doesn't matter, you guys," Harper said. "We need to go."

We hurried out of the room just in time to hear shouts and arguing.

"But you have to give it to me!" Hercules yelled. His voice boomed around the entire volcanic chamber.

The grouchy guy grumbled something, except he grumbled it really loud. It sounded a lot like a bunch of reasons why Hercules shouldn't order him around, including the fact that Hercules didn't have an appointment.

Hercules shouted again and then stormed toward the exit. Except if he left now, there was literally no way for him not to see us.

"In here," Harper said, ducking into a different tunnel in the side of the path.

We followed her into a smooth tunnel that was almost perfectly round.

"What is this place?" I said.

"Lava tube," she said. "If we follow it, it should lead us out."

That was the best plan we had. She led the way and we followed, and sure enough, we finally came to the surface. Once we were out, I turned back to look.

There was no sign of the opening we'd just come through. Somehow it was hidden from our eyes.

"You still have it?" I said.

Harper held the golden knife up. "Got it!"

The crown felt hot against my stomach, but I didn't mention it.

"Then let's go back to Prometheus right now," I said.

"Now?" Daniel said.

"Yeah, why not?"

"Because it's like midnight and there are scary creatures out?" he said.

And almost like they heard him, hooves started pounding

in the distance, coming closer.

"This way," I said, turned away from the pounding hooves. But that was no better. The snort of the giant boar filled the air. The worst part about both was that we couldn't see any of the monsters because it was so dark, but I was willing to bet that they could see us.

Harper bit her lip. "I vote that we wait until daylight."

As brave as Harper was, I knew this was the best idea.

"Fine," I said. "But we're going first chance we get."

# CHAPTER 30

I decided to wake up at five. Instead I woke up at seven o'clock to Jason shouting at the top of his lungs.

"Wake up, Campers! We have a busy day."

I rubbed my eyes to get every bit of sleep out of them, but with the late night before, I was taking a nap if I got even ten minutes of a chance today.

*A ten minute nap now for ten minutes off your life*, a voice in my mind said.

It was the Fates. Or it was my mind pretending to be the Fates.

"No way," I said. But I guess I said it aloud.

"Did you just say no to me?" Jason asked, getting in my face.

I shook my head. "Of course not. Let's hunt the Hydra."

I didn't want to leave the golden crown in the bunk, so

I tucked it under my shirt. Since our bunk was packed, and since Hercules had eaten everything in sight, we each got a cereal bar for breakfast.

*Bacon and eggs for seven minutes off your life,* the Fates said again.

I ignored them. Like I was going to trade time off my life for breakfast.

Well, maybe if the eggs were sunny-side up, the bacon was extra crispy, and there was Texas toast on the side.

No, of course not. That would be ridiculous.

Still, I tried to pretend my cereal bar was bacon even though it tasted like dried-up wheat bread.

Daniel looked about the same as me, with tired eyes and bed-head, but Harper appeared completely ready for the day. We fell to the back as soon as we got outside. Jason and Atty were up front, telling everyone in our bunk what to do.

Mia glanced back at us, like she knew we were up to something. I motioned for her to come back and join us.

"Can you cover for us again today?" I said.

"Again?" Mia said. "You didn't get the fire yet?"

I shook my head. "There were complications."

Mia scowled. "You know, I almost had to lie for you guys yesterday. It was like Atty knew something was up. When I came in at the end of the day, she asked where you were."

At her words, I swear Atty looked over. She couldn't have heard. She was probably just mad that we were talking when she was talking. Atty did not like to be interrupted.

"And what'd you say?" Daniel whispered. He looked really worried, and I get that he didn't want to get in trouble, but this was a matter of life or death.

"I said you guys were just really slow and couldn't keep up with me," Mia said.

I almost laughed except then I realized it was kind of insulting, but whatever. She did cover for us.

"Just today, one more time," I said. "I promise."

Mia looked to Harper who nodded.

"We really have to go," Harper said.

Mia blew out a breath. "Fine. One more time. But that's it."

The plan was the same as yesterday except our bunk was heading deeper into the forest, farther away from Mount Olympus. We split off from Mia and doubled back once we were out of sight and took the same route to Mount Olympus, and lucky us, we climbed the mountain just in time to see one of the eagles swooping in for its daily snack.

But it got really annoyed and kept pecking and pecking. Prometheus started laughing a giant guffaw that I figured every single person at camp could probably hear. Finally, the eagle hissed at him and flew away, back to the top of the column where its mate was. They both watched us like hawks. I mean like eagles.

"We're back," I said as we got closer to him.

Prometheus grinned like everything in the world was finally going his way. "Did you see them? Did you?"

"The eagles?" I asked.

"Yes, the eagles! They couldn't get through the bandana! It was a thing of beauty."

Harper glanced up at the birds. "They might come back."

Prometheus leaned his head back. "Let them try!" he shouted.

I get that he was happy and all, but there was no reason to tempt the birds to come back.

"Oh, by the way, I have the worst itch," Prometheus said. "Can you scratch just below my left elbow? It's horrible. I can't take it anymore."

His elbow was covered in dirt and hair, and the last thing I wanted to do was touch him. I looked to Daniel who shook his head. Harper stepped back and got really busy tying her shoes.

"Fine." I stepped forward and scratched just below his left elbow.

From the sounds Prometheus made, you would have thought he was eating popcorn with extra butter.

What I wouldn't give for popcorn with butter. Except all we had was cereal bars. And we still had five weeks left of summer camp. I had no idea how that was going to work out, especially if Hercules kept eating all the food.

"Now over my right eye," he said.

I scratched over his eye. Then he mentioned his left foot. I stopped scratching. I wanted to save the world, but no way was I touching some gross old Titan foot.

"We brought something to free you," I said.

All complaints of itches disappeared, and his eyes narrowed.

"If this is some little kid joke, it's not funny," Prometheus said. "I swear I'll call up to Zeus right now and have him send you to Tartarus if you're messing with me."

"We're not messing with you," Harper said, and she pulled the knife from her backpack.

Prometheus stared at it and didn't say a word. Harper flipped it around so he could see all sides. The sun hit on it perfectly, making it shine in the morning light.

"Where did you get it?" Prometheus asked, but then said, "No, don't tell me. The less I know, the better. Just cut these stupid chains."

Harper didn't move. "You remember our deal, right?"

Daniel smacked her. "You don't question the gods."

"Sure I do," Harper said. "What if he plans to run away and not give us immortal fire? What then?"

Prometheus cleared his throat. "I wouldn't do that. If you free me, then I'll give you immortal fire that will never go out."

His eyes hadn't left the knife.

"You promise?" Harper said. "Because we are really putting ourselves on the line here."

"I promise."

She moved to where his giant hand was and held up her other hand. "Pinky promise. Say that you will give us the fire."

"Pinky promise?" Prometheus said. "What is that?"

She put her little finger up and interlocked it with his enormous finger. "This is a pinky promise. And the penalty for breaking a pinky promise is twenty years in Tartarus."

I figured she was making that part up, but it sounded pretty good.

Prometheus tightened his pinky. "I pinky promise."

Harper winced, because I guess he was holding on pretty

tight. Harper said, "Promise made. It can't be broken."

They let go and Harper placed the golden knife next to the chain holding his right hand. She inserted it into the top link and made a sawing motion.

It cut right through the metal!

"Whoa! It works!" Daniel said. "That awesome!"

Prometheus pulled his now free right hand around to look at it. Sheer disbelief covered his face. But if I'd been chained to a mountain for thousands of years, I'd be pretty excited about getting freed, too.

She cut the chain by his right foot next, then his left foot, and then finally his left arm. At the final cut, both eagles jumped from their perch and dove for us. We flattened ourselves to the ground and used my shield for cover. They swooped over. Then they flew off, toward the top of Mount Olympus.

"You did it," Prometheus said. "You kids really did it."

Harper shoved the knife in her backpack, which I was happy about. After stealing it, I didn't want Prometheus to take it from us.

"Now the fire," Daniel said. He held the olive branch out, but kind of mumbled the words like he still didn't want to ask this Titan for a favor. But seriously, we'd just freed him from having his liver eaten each day. Fire was the least he could do for us.

"Zeus will not be happy," Prometheus said, looking up toward the clouds.

"Yeah, a lot of people aren't happy right now," I said.

"Can we please just get the fire?" Daniel said, waving the

branch the smallest amount.

This seemed to get Prometheus' attention. He reached with one of his giant hands and placed it over the end of the branch. It burst into flames.

He pulled his hand back. I guess he was immune to fire.

"So that's it?" Harper said.

"That's it." Prometheus stood, towering over us. And by towering, I mean that he seemed to have grown even bigger than he was. His head was as tall as the column the eagles had perched on. "If you cup your hand over the flame, it will disappear."

"Wait, you said it would never go out," Harper said.

"It won't," Prometheus said. "You can reignite it by placing your hand back over the top of it. The fire will last forever."

I felt like he was leaving out a key piece of information. "Will that work for all three of us?" I asked.

"Just him," Prometheus said, pointing a giant hand at Daniel. "And if you don't mind, I'll be on my way."

Just Daniel? I guess it would have to do.

"Do we get a thank you?" Harper asked.

I elbowed her. I may not know much about mythology, but I had a pretty good idea that the gods didn't run around thanking mere mortals like us.

But Prometheus dropped to one knee and bowed his head. "You three have more than my thanks. I owe you a debt. Remember that. When you need it, call for me, and I'll help. I swear it."

Wow. Just wow. I was not expecting that.

We all stood there speechless as Prometheus stood up and ran away. And because he was so tall, it didn't take him many steps to vanish from sight.

"Oh, wait, you still have my bandana!" I yelled.

"You should have asked him for it earlier," Harper said. "It's not like he can hear you now."

I blew out a breath. I'd have to suffer the wrath of Jason and Atty and ask for a new one once things settled down.

We hurried down Mount Olympus.

"Now we just have to find our bunkmates and find the Hydra," I said when we got to Lucky Rock.

"Why aren't you at your posts?" someone said.

We turned toward the flagpole. There was Atty, arms crossed, looking like she'd eaten vinegar for breakfast.

It didn't matter now. I grabbed the torch from Daniel and held it out. "We got immortal fire, to help defeat the Hydra. It's the only fire that will work."

She narrowed her eyes. "How do you know that? And where did you get this fire?"

I wasn't sure which question to answer first, or if I even needed to answer both of them.

"Prometheus?" I said, unsure if I should mention it. I didn't want to get him in trouble.

Her eyes looked upward, toward Mount Olympus. "Prometheus? The Titan? And he just gave this immortal fire to you?"

"Not exactly," I said, and I gave her the short version that skipped the part about us stealing a weapon from Hephaestus.

Atty's eyes got darker with each word from my mouth.

"You freed a Titan?" she said.

"Well, yeah," I said. "It was the only way to get the immortal fire."

"And you didn't think that would be a problem?"

I'll admit that I hadn't thought that far.

"Is it a problem?" I said.

Fury filled Atty's eyes. "Yeah, Logan, it's a big problem. Zeus is going to be furious."

At her words, thunder rumbled around us, and a giant streak of lightning shot out, striking Lucky Rock. It sizzled and turned the golden rock completely black.

"We have to go," Atty said. "But this is not over. There will be consequences."

None of us questioned her. We just followed her as she ran.

"You don't make Zeus angry!" Atty shouted as soon as we were inside the trees.

"But we need the fire," I said. "What were we supposed to do?"

She whipped around and faced me. "You were supposed to follow directions, Logan. That's what you were supposed to do."

I still held the torch, and even with her being so mad, I didn't regret us getting it.

She was about to open her mouth and yell at us some more when Jason came running up.

"We found the Hydra!" he said.

He was completely out of breath and looked like half his ponytail has been torn off.

"Where?" Atty said.

"By the caves. We've got her surrounded."

# CHAPTER 31

Everything was a blur as we ran for the caves. Jason led the way, tearing through the trees faster than I'd ever imagined. We all kept up, even Daniel. And then the trees cleared away, and there was the rest of our bunk, including Mia, surrounding the monster.

The Hydra looked even bigger than when we'd seen it before. All ten heads were red and shiny and darting down from one camper to the next. Kids jumped out of the way.

"Is anyone hurt?" Jason called.

"Everyone's fine," Mia said.

Except the words weren't even all the way out of her mouth when the Hydra snaked its head down and grabbed this kid named Henry around the waist.

Jason and Atty were there before the teeth could sink in. Atty swung her sword and it sliced through the head so neatly that it almost looked fake. But we'd done this before. If I didn't act right now, two more heads would grow in its place.

I ran forward and shoved the torch down where the head had been. It smelled gross. I wasn't going to stay here longer than I needed to. After a good five seconds, I jumped back.

Henry was just getting to his feet. "I'm dying!" he whined.

Atty looked him over. "You're fine. Stop your complaining."

It looked like his shirt had protected him from the Hydra's teeth.

"Nice work with the fire!" Jason said. "Where'd you get it? We've tried fire three other times and it hasn't worked."

Sure enough, the Hydra had thirteen heads instead of ten. Well, now only twelve since Atty had just cut one off.

Atty snarled. "They freed Prometheus."

"What!?" Jason said.

"Not now," Harper shouted. "It's attacking again."

And so for the next hour we battled the Hydra until the last head was gone.

"The mortal head," Jason said, picking it up. "Why did it have to be the last one?"

"Guess somebody didn't touch Lucky Rock today," I said.

Jason shot me a look of death. "Yeah, I guess not. And if I ever catch you guys breaking the rules again, I swear I'll haul you off to Tartarus myself."

I put on my best innocent look. "I don't think we broke any rules, at least not technically." Sure, we'd been out after curfew to steal the knife from Hephaestus, but Jason and Atty didn't need to know about that.

He scowled. "Camp Rule Number Thirteen: Do not free a Titan."

I rolled my eyes. "That is not Camp Rule Number Thirteen."

"It is now," Atty said. "Because freeing a Titan is very bad luck, just like the number thirteen."

"But we didn't—" I started.

"Be quiet, Logan," Jason said. He threw the head at me. I caught it easily, just like a football. But instead of a football, it was all squishy and gross, and I got stuff all over my hands.

"Now what do we do?" Mia said.

"Now we—" Atty started, but Daniel cut her off.

"Look at the Hydra!"

We all turned to look. I wished I hadn't. The entire thing sunk into the ground, like it was being reabsorbed. A chill ran through me. This was not good. This was definitely not good.

"We need to check on the other teams," Atty said. Or at least I think that's what she said, but her words got all fuzzy in my head, like they were tripping all over each other.

"Come on, Logan." Harper pulled on my arm.

I tried to take a step, but it didn't work like I thought it would, and my knee buckled under me.

"What's wrong with him?" Daniel said. He looked terrified.

"He's turning purple," Mia said. "Why is he turning purple?"

The entire world swam around me, and my other knee buckled. Jason was down, looking in my face.

"Why isn't your bandana on, Logan?" he shouted.

The words hurt my head. Bandana? That's right. Bandana. Prometheus. The Hydra . . . something about the Hydra, but my mind wasn't working.

I fell over and something rolled out of my arms. I blinked a couple times, just enough to see the mortal head of the Hydra staring back at me. Then the world went black.

# CHAPTER 32

I woke up to about fifteen people staring back at me. I was shivering, but it felt like I was under a thick blanket.

"What's up?" I managed to say. Or at least that's what I tried to say, but my tongue felt really thick, like a giant wad of bubble gum.

Atty's face appeared in front of me. She looked like she was ready to scream and was barely holding it back.

"Logan, what is Camp Rule Number Three?" she asked.

Camp Rule?

That's right. I was at Camp Hercules. We'd just fought the Hydra. Then . . . well, that's where it got a little fuzzy.

"Um . . . ," I started.

"Wear your T-shirt and bandana at all times," Daniel said, coming into view.

I looked down at my yellow T-shirt. But I couldn't see

my neck where my bandana was supposed to be. And then I remembered that I'd given it to Prometheus.

"Oh. I . . ." I didn't want to mentioned that I'd not only freed a Titan, but that I'd given him a magical bandana that would help protect him.

"You what?"

"I need a new one. I lost my other one."

"You messed up," Atty said. "And when you finish healing, I may kill you myself."

"You wouldn't do that," I mumbled. But then again, this was Atty we were talking about.

"The fleece worked," Harper said, popping into my vision. "That's so cool."

Jason lifted the warm blanket off me, but I'd stopped shivering so I didn't mind. It was actually getting kind of toasty under there. That combined with Texas weather, and I'd be sweating in a couple seconds.

"Of course it worked. That's one of its powers."

"Yeah, but still, it's really awesome. You should wear it around." Harper went to grab it, but Jason pulled it far out of her reach.

"Nope," Jason said. "The fleece stays here."

His campfire story came back to be, about how he'd gone in search of this Golden Fleece. It was nice to know that it had a practical use, too.

Jason disappeared from sight, I guess to put the fleece wherever he kept it. Probably hanging on a hook in his room, just like Atty's apples were sitting on a shelf, tempting everyone who happened to see them.

I crawled out of bed and felt for the golden crown. It was still there, under my shirt. I don't know why I cared so much about it, but I also didn't want to let anyone else know about it.

*Don't trust anyone.* The words of the Fates came back to me. Maybe the crown is what they were talking about. Maybe I was supposed to keep it secret, even from Daniel and Harper.

My stomach rumbled like I hadn't eaten in fifty days, so I headed for the kitchen. Daniel and Harper trailed after me, but all I could think about was potato chips and pizza. I threw open the pantry door.

"It's empty," I said.

"Yeah, the other bunks have been eating a lot," Daniel said. "All that's left is oatmeal." He grabbed a packet of instant oatmeal and shoved it my way.

I didn't bother with water. I tore it open and upending it into my mouth.

"I need more food," I said.

He gave me another packet. But I was still hungry. We needed to get these labors under control and rebuild the dining hall or I was going to starve to death.

"How'd the other bunks do?" I asked. My mouth was super dry, so I filled a glass with water and downed it.

Harper raised her hand and started counting off on her fingers. "Team Lion managed to herd the lion into a cave, but no one wants to go in because they're scared."

"We're not scared," some kid in a red T-shirt said. He must've been on Team Lion.

Harper rolled her eyes. "Team Hind managed to capture the Hind. Team Boar didn't even come close to capturing the boar. Team Cow Stable is still at it."

"They asked for help, but Jason used you as an excuse," Daniel said. "So we owe you one. Otherwise we'd be stuck mucking out cow poop until midnight."

"You're welcome," I said.

Harper continued. "Team Bird has gotten a lot of those birds, but they won't stop coming."

Atty came running by and yelled, "They're regenerating, way too fast. The Hydra confirmed it. They shouldn't be coming back this quickly. But they are."

She ran off, and we hurried after her.

Atty didn't stop in the great room. Instead, she ran out front to the stone patio where Hercules stood.

I ducked as a bird flew over my head. But it didn't attack. Then another flew over. Then at least twenty. None of them even looked at us. The giant boar charged by next, tearing out of the woods and running past the bunk. Then, the Amazon women rode by on their horses. They didn't glance our way.

Other kids started filing out of the bunk, because with all the noise from the monsters and things running by, it was obvious that something was up.

Hercules stopped talking the second he saw me. He stared at me, like he wasn't quite sure who I was. But that was weird. I'd returned Cerberus to the Underworld. He knew me.

"You're different," he finally said, standing tall with his hands on his hips.

"I got hurt. But I'm fine." I didn't need Hercules knowing about the bandana and Prometheus. Not now.

"What's going on?" Harper said, pushing her way up to where Atty and Hercules stood. Jason hurried out to join them along with most of the other counselors.

Atty said something, but no one could hear because a herd of cattle ran by, pounding their hooves on the ground so loudly my bones rattled.

I was about to say something, but then I saw Cerberus. He came out from the trees, running toward base camp. When he saw Harper, Daniel, and me, he let out three quick barks, one with each of his three heads. Then he kept running until he was out of sight.

"The labors are respawning immediately," Atty said to Hercules. "We can't fight them this way."

He clenched his teeth and blew out a deep breath. "It's our worst fear. Without the amphora to control them, Hera's curse rules them. And with the added strength from being stored in the amphora, they're too strong. They will continue to regenerate over and over again. We have no control."

Daniel put his head in his hands. "So we're going to have to fight the Hydra constantly? I can't do that all summer. There has to be something we can do about this."

"There's nothing," Hercules said. "I was not able to get a new amphora. And since the labors are all here, inside Camp Hercules, we will have to stay here forever fighting them. I'm counting on you campers. I'm sorry that our fates are now intertwined, but this is your destiny. It will be a good life. A noble life. Your families will be proud."

He had to be kidding. Fight the same monsters over and over and over again? And it wasn't like it would stop when summer camp was over. This was going to go on forever. I was going to be stuck at Camp Hercules for the rest of my life—which may be cut short only if the Hydra managed to eat me.

Just then, Achilles ran up. He waved his arms like a crazy person.

"The gate!" he shouted "The gate!"

"The gate is secured and needs to stay that way," Hercules said. "That is our destiny."

"No!" Achilles shouted. "Someone unlocked it. We've been trying to close it, but it's no use. The labors are escaping into the outer world."

 **CHAPTER 33**

Escaping into the outer world! That meant Mom was at risk. This was the worst thing ever.

"Who opened it?" Jason shouted. He grabbed his sword like he was ready to do battle right then and there.

"We don't know," Achilles said. "We found it open. The Cretan Bull had already left camp."

"I'll tell you who opened it," Hercules said. He seemed to stand a foot taller and his face darkened. "It is a minion of Hera, my evil stepmother. That is who is behind it."

Atty bit her lip. "So there is a spy, right here in camp."

I felt my defensive barriers go up. *Don't trust anyone.* The spy could be anyone. Anywhere. In any of the bunks.

"If anyone has seen anything suspicious, it needs to be reported immediately," Hercules said.

"What kind of suspicious?" Daniel asked. He was

probably hoping that no one would tattle on us about sneaking off to Mount Olympus to see Prometheus.

Mia looked like she was about to open her mouth, so I tried to catch her eye. She wouldn't look at me.

"Anyone going off alone," Hercules said. "Acting strangely. Communicating with anyone outside of camp."

Some kid in Team Horse raised his hand. "I saw Divya walking off alone earlier today."

A girl a couple people over from him stomped her foot. "I was not alone, idiot. I was meeting with the old ladies who run the Trading Post."

"Why?" the kid said.

"None of your business," she said.

She had to be talking about the Fates. They'd probably sold her something.

Four other kids ratted out their friends for things like drinking water from some river that had been talking to them, trying to steal some pomegranates from the Garden of Persephone, and—here's the worst—trying to get some privacy to use the bathroom. This was horrible. Everyone was turning on everyone.

Then I remembered on our way back from Mount Olympus that Harper had gone off alone. And she'd headed right toward the gate.

But no. That was ridiculous. I was not going to rat her out. Except she hadn't told us what she was doing.

Still, she wasn't working for Hera.

Except there was the part about her only reason for being here at camp being to spy for her mom.

Ugh. The back and forth in my mind made my brain hurt.

I bit my lip and glanced at Daniel. It looked like he was thinking the same thing as me. But no way was I going to say a word. I'd deal with this on my own.

"So what do we do?" Mia said.

Hercules looked to the sky. "Campers, I must ask you to prepare for battle."

# CHAPTER 34

"We can still shut the gate!" Jason said. He took off running for the front gate of Camp Hercules, shield and sword in his hands.

"Team Hydra, stay here," Atty said. She ran after him.

I looked to Harper and Daniel. "Guys, we have to get out of that gate before they close it."

Daniel looked at me like my brain was still asleep back in our bunk. "Get out the gate? With the monsters?"

Yeah, sure, it wasn't like I was crazy excited about leaving Camp Hercules to go fight monsters in the real world, but if there were monsters out there, then we had to do something about them. The world was at risk. Mom was in danger.

Harper smacked Daniel on the arm. "You heard Hercules. He told us we have prepare for battle. That means getting out the gate to fight the monsters that have escaped."

"Yeah," Daniel said. "But Atty told us to stay here. And we don't know which monsters have left yet. What if the Hydra is still here inside the walls of Camp Hercules?"

I grabbed his arm and started dragging him toward our bunk. "The Hydra doesn't matter. Any of the monsters can hurt our friends and families."

"But we're Team Hydra which means we fight the Hydra," Daniel said. His words sounded a lot less sure as the seconds passed. Too many seconds. We had to get moving.

I looked Daniel right in the eyes. "Daniel, we are Team Hercules. We have to help, no matter what." I tried to sound all important when I said it, and I guess I did pretty well, because after about ten seconds, Daniel nodded.

"Okay. We'll go fight the monsters," he said.

Since camp was in complete chaos, nobody was watching us. Nobody except Harper's roommate Mia.

"What are you guys doing?" she asked as we grabbed our weapons from the bunk.

I hooked my sword and spear on and grabbed my shield.

"We're leaving camp," Harper said. "Are you coming?"

Mia didn't hesitate. "I'm coming." She grabbed her stuff, and the four of us ran for the front gate.

When we got there, Hercules stood on top of the fence, the same place he'd been the day we arrived.

Most of the demigod counselors stood against the gate, trying to close it. Jason led the effort, yelling when everyone was supposed to push on the gate.

"It's not closed yet," I said, as we ran up.

"No, Logan," Atty said, whipping her head around at the

sound of my voice. "It's not closed yet. And why are you here when I specifically asked you to stay back by the bunk?"

"We wanted to help," I said, though that was the opposite of what I planned to do.

"Why's it taking so long to close it?" Harper said. "It's not that heavy."

Her words made my brain itch. How would Harper know how heavy the gate was unless she was the one who'd opened it in the first place? But no. Harper was not Hera's spy. She couldn't be.

Except she could be. Anyone could me. Except me. I knew I wasn't a spy.

"Push!" Jason yelled, and everyone pushed. But a bunch of cows ran out of the trees near the left and barreled into the counselors, sending them sprawling. What progress they'd made closing the gate vanished. The cows had pushed it back open. Then the cows ran out beyond the barrier of Camp Hercules.

"That's why it's not closed yet," Atty said. "The labors are keeping it open."

"So they can all escape, right?" Daniel said.

"It's like they're working together," Atty said, throwing a rock after the cows. It hit one on the butt, making it jump. But the cow kept going, until the entire bunch of them was out of sight.

"We need to get out there," I said. I wasn't sure why I said it aloud, since we'd been trying to sneak out. But it just came out, and then there was no taking it back.

Atty looked right at me. Here it came. She was going to

tell me all the reasons why I had no idea what I was talking about.

"Just be careful and don't get yourself killed," Atty said.

Wait. What? She was agreeing with me? That made no sense at all.

"Push!" Jason yelled again.

I glanced over. They'd made really good progress with the gate this time. If we didn't move, we wouldn't make it.

"You're going to let us go?" Daniel said.

"Someone needs to be out there," Atty said. "And we might as well send our best."

My mouth dropped open. The best? I had to have heard wrong.

"And we're on that list?" I finally managed to say.

Atty put a hand on my arm. "Logan, don't ever ask me to repeat this, but you guys are at the top of my list."

I tried really hard to keep the smile off my face, since with the whole monster situation, everything was pretty serious right now, but how cool was that? Atty thought we were the best.

"Are you coming?" Harper asked.

Atty shook her head. "Jason and I are going back to Hephaestus, to get a replacement amphora. Now go!"

I did not need to be told twice. I ran for the gate. Harper, Daniel, and Mia followed. The counselors almost had the gate closed, but we passed through before it finally slammed shut behind us. We were outside the walls of Camp Hercules.

## CHAPTER 35

"op of the list. Did you hear that?" I was going to bask in the glory of that compliment for the rest of my life.

"She wasn't just talking about you," Harper said. "She meant all of us."

"I'll share my glory," I said. "I was getting kind of tired of looking down at you guys anyway."

Harper rolled her eyes but didn't bother responding.

"You guys live nearby?" Mia said.

Oh yeah. Back to the real world. We were out here for a reason. I needed to get to my house to see Mom. And Daniel only lived a few houses away from me.

"About five miles away," I said. "What about you?"

Mia blinked a few times, like she had something in her eye. "I don't live close."

That was kind of obvious by her response, but it was also a little evasive. Maybe she lived on Mars and didn't want to admit to being an alien.

"Harper lives in DC," Daniel said. "Her mom's a reporter. She used to have a really cool camera pen, but Charon took it away in the Underworld."

Mia had to know this already—well except for the camera pen thing. She was Harper's roommate after all. But Daniel had a hard time shutting up around Mia.

"The real Charon?" Mia said. Her eyes got huge. "When did you meet him?"

The way she said it made me not want to tell her. But that was silly. Harper trusted her, so why shouldn't I?

"Logan dragged us to the Underworld to return Cerberus," Harper said. "And all I was trying to do was take a few pictures of the place. Like that's a crime."

"That's so unfair," Mia said. "Charon sounds like a jerk."

"No way," Daniel said. "He was epic. He—"

"Enough chitchat," I said, cutting him off. "We need to get to my house." But then the reality set in. Five miles was a long way to go.

"An ideas on how to get there?" I had zero cash, no idea if there was a bus that even stopped near my house, and sure didn't have an Uber app. I didn't even have a phone.

"We could call our moms," Daniel said, holding up a phone.

I grabbed it. "You have a phone? How is that possible?"

Daniel pulled it out of my hand. "My mom says it's good for emergencies."

"This is an emergency," Mia said. "You should call her and get her to pick us up."

But Harper shook her head. "I don't think that's a good idea."

As much as I didn't want to walk the five miles to our houses, I had to agree with her.

"Harper's right," I said. "We need to look for signs of the monsters while we're out here."

Daniel cringed. "So you're saying we have to walk five miles?"

I nodded.

"In the heat?"

He had a point. This was Texas in the summer. It was already one hundred degrees at least. And even though my camp T-shirt was keeping me kind of cool, I was still sweating so much, it was like I'd just taken a shower.

"In the heat," I said.

"What about sunburn?" Daniel said.

I guess he didn't pack any sunscreen. "You can pull up your bandana," I suggested. I didn't think he would, but he immediately did, making him look like some kind of Wild West bank robber.

It didn't take us long to find the first sign of the labors.

"What's that horrible smell?" I said.

Mia pointed to a high school football field we were walking by. Fifty cows grazed in the grass, and there were five piles of cow poop stacked up around them.

"Guess we found where the Cattle of Geryon are," Daniel said.

"Good thing it's not football season," I said. But that only reminded me that I'd wanted to go to football camp during the summer, not to a mythology camp. And sure, Camp Hercules had been fun, but if we didn't fix this labor problem, I'd be spending the rest of my life as a member of Camp Hercules, battling monsters.

Daniel edged over to the fence to get a better look at them. "Do we try to capture them and bring them back to camp?"

"We could totally do it," Harper said. "We'd just need to tie them all together and lead them."

"You do a lot of cattle rustling back in DC?" I asked.

Harper shrugged. "I went to pioneer camp last summer. My mom was sure there was something funny going on there, so she sent me to investigate."

Harper's mom was either a really good reporter or just super nosy.

"They aren't hurting anything here," I said. "And it doesn't look like they're going anywhere. We should keep moving."

I'd seen enough of these labors in the last couple weeks to know that some of them were inconvenient and some were huge problems, like the Hydra. The Hydra tried to eat people. That was way worse than cows going to the bathroom at the rival high school.

Further down the road we saw a bunch of news people running frantically around the local McDonald's with cameras and microphones. Apparently some giant birds had torn down the golden arches and stolen all the French Fries.

"Hey, look, you guys," Harper said. "It was the Stymphalian birds." She shoved her way right into the middle of the news crews and pulled a couple feathers from a nearby tree. They were red, and made of metal.

"Don't touch the end," Daniel said, almost grabbing them from her. "It's poison."

Harper rolled her eyes. "I know that. I was there when they attacked. Remember?"

"You should leave them here," Daniel said. "They're too dangerous."

Harper completely ignored him, shoving them into her back pocket. "They might come in handy."

She had a good point. I looked around for more of the feathers, but didn't see any. Mia found one under an upended stack of trays at the outdoor play area.

We kept going, down the road. Arrows covered the wall and roof of the local Starbucks. A giant boar had torn through the grocery store. And people were running out of a shopping mall, saying Amazon women had taken over and were riding horses through the department stores. Pretty much the entire city had gone crazy.

I thought that was the worst of it, but then we walked in the front door of my house. Mom was sitting at the kitchen table, having a cup of coffee with the goddess Athena.

# CHAPTER 36

**M**om and Athena? Having coffee together? I had about a million things I wanted to ask, like how did they know each other, and why was Athena here. But I never got the chance to ask any of my questions because something enormous landed on the roof. The entire house shook.

My hand immediately went to my sword. Guess the last two weeks of hero training had done me some good after all. But Mom . . . well, there was no easy way to explain what happened next.

Mom reached up to the top of the refrigerator and grabbed our old fly swatter. She said like two words, and it turned into a sword. Then Athena grabbed a sword off her back, and the time for words was over.

Whatever was on the roof started clawing its way down

the shingles. Outside the window, huge chunks of our roof fell over the side, and then the monster jumped and landed in our front yard.

"It's the Nemean Lion!" Daniel shouted. He grabbed his shield and shuffled behind me, into the family room. Harper grabbed her circle chakram thing and clenched it in her fist. Mia raised her spear, like she was ready to throw it.

The lion was taller than our house, but it lowered its head so it could see right inside the window. Drool dripped from its mouth because its fangs were so gigantic that they didn't fit inside. Its eyes were bright red, like lasers. I stopped looking at them because I had this weird feeling that they could burn right through my soul.

"Stay behind me, Logan," Mom said, and she darted

toward the window, holding her fly swatter sword in front of herself.

"Are you kidding?" I said. "You stay behind me. What are even doing? What is that?"

"Later," Mom said, and then she attacked.

Mom and Athena jumped out the window, spraying glass all over the rocks in our front yard. I made a mental note to not go out there barefooted. Athena lunged forward and swung her sword at the lion. Mom did, too, and her sword connected with the lion's shoulder. Then she struck again. And again.

"Your mom is awesome," Harper said.

Yeah, she was pretty awesome. Except the cuts from her sword didn't make a scratch.

Harper flicked her wrist, and her chakram sliced through the air. It hit the lion, but bounced off, falling to the ground. Mia did the same with her spear. But nothing seemed to work.

"Mortal weapons won't work on the lion," Daniel yelled from behind us.

That was just great.

"What are we supposed to do?" I tossed the worthless sword aside. But I grabbed my shield. Hopefully it would protect me from the monster.

Mia yanked a tray with two owls on it from our kitchen wall. "We need to distract it. Then maybe Athena can kill it."

"With a tray?" I said.

But Mia was one step ahead of me. She turned the tray sideways, like a Frisbee, and tossed it at the lion. I grabbed a bunch of plates and jumped out the window, handing half to

Harper and keeping half myself. Mom was not going to be happy, but I could worry about that later.

One after another, Harper and I tossed plates at the Nemean Lion from the side. Mia stayed inside, but did the same, using bowls and forks and teacups. At first, the lion didn't even react, but we kept at it, like an annoying fly, and finally it whipped around to face us.

The lion roared so loudly that I dropped my shield in an effort to cover my ears. Then it lowered itself to the ground and snarled. Harper and I were in serious trouble since there was no way we could fight the thing.

That's when Athena attacked. She ran up and sliced her sword right through the middle of the lion. Blood and guts spewed everywhere, and it fell to the ground in two pieces. Its mouth was five inches away from me. Five inches. I was seriously almost dead.

I kicked at the stupid lion and threw the final plate at it. Then the lion shimmered and shifted and sank into the ground, disappearing from our front yard, just like the Hydra had done back at camp.

# CHAPTER 37

"What was that?" I shouted. Not the lion. Not it disappearing. I'd seen that before. But what about the fact that it was here, right where I was going: my own house?

"Wait until we're inside, Logan," Mom said, and she motioned with her head.

Oh, yeah. We weren't back at camp. And even though on a normal day we never saw our neighbors, every single neighbor as far as I could see stood outside watching. Every single one except Daniel's mom, that was.

"Hi," I said, waving at the neighbors since most held up their cell phones, like they'd recorded the entire thing. A couple waved back. Then we all headed inside.

"What about my mom?" Daniel said. "Where is she?" He'd managed to come out of the family room and back into the kitchen. Huge streaks of sunlight poured through the roof where the Nemean Lion had ripped holes in it. That was going to be pretty inconvenient if it rained.

Mom handed Daniel a soda from the fridge. "She's fine. I suggested she leave town for the week."

"You did?" Daniel said. "Why would you do that?"

Mom motioned at the roof, the yard, the broken window. "Because this was coming."

"But how did you know this was coming?" I said. "And what is she doing here?" I pointed to Athena who smiled at me in return.

"You're my favorite goddess, by the way," Mia said. She took the soda that Mom offered her.

Athena actually didn't look very flattered. "You told me that the last time we met."

It didn't sound so much like flattery this time around, more like Mia was trying to be a teacher's pet.

"Oh, yeah, I guess I did," Mia said, then she sat at the table.

I finally grabbed a soda for myself and passed one to Harper, and we sat down. An owl flew through one of the holes in the roof and landed on Athena's shoulder. Mom didn't act like any of this was the least bit weird.

She held the sword out in front of her, said a couple words, and it changed back into a fly swatter. Then she put it back on top of the fridge. I'd used that thing to swat bugs before. No way was it a sword. Except it was.

"Okay, what's going on?" I said. "Why is Athena here?"

Mom smiled at Athena. "We're sisters. Didn't you know

that?"

I opened my mouth but nothing came out. Sisters? How was I supposed to know that? I didn't know anything about this mythology stuff. Except . . . I had always known who Athena was. Mom had mentioned her as being a Greek goddess lots of times. And there was the owl fascination that Mom had. We had owls all over our house.

"No way!" Daniel said. "You aunt is Athena? That is so cool."

"My aunt's not Athena," I said. "Is she?"

Mom nodded, and Athena said, "It's true. We're sisters. Well, you know, half-sisters."

"But how?" I said to Mom. "You don't have any sisters or brothers."

Mom scrunched up her face like she was thinking. "I guess when I told you that, I wasn't being completely honest."

"Oh really?" I said. "You think it was a little bit of a lie to forget to mention your sister is a goddess?"

"People keep all kinds of secrets," Harper said. "That's what my mom tells me. She says that when you root out the secrets, that's when the juiciest news comes out. Just wait until I tell her about this."

Both Mom and Athena fixed their eyes on Harper. "That can't happen," Athena said. "One word to your mother and—"

"And what?" Harper said.

Was she seriously challenging a goddess?

"Don't test me," Athena said.

Daniel had enough soda to finally rejoin the conversation.

"Too bad Charon threw your camera away in the Underworld," he said. "Otherwise you could have gotten a picture of the lion. That would make an amazing Instagram post."

With all the neighbors who'd been watching, I was willing to bet that it already had.

Harper crossed her arms. "I still want my camera back. Can you get it for me?" she asked Athena.

"Absolutely not," Athena said.

My head still spun from this new information, and I had no idea how it was even possible. Mom had said that her mother died before I was born. But I'd met her dad a bunch of times.

"So Grandpa . . . ," I started.

"Your grandfather is Zeus," Mom said, like it was the most normal thing in the universe.

"Grandpa is Zeus?" I said. He came to visit us probably once a month. Our big outings were either McDonald's or the movies. He always let me get popcorn refills.

"We don't mention it," Mom said. "Hera doesn't like to be reminded of it."

"It probably makes her furious!" Daniel said. "Hera getting mad is the whole reason Hercules got in trouble with these labors."

Athena drained her coffee cup, which had somehow been left untouched during the entire Nemean Lion battle. "Hera is the whole reason the entire world is in danger right now. She's really gone too far this time."

Mom refilled her coffee. "And Hera is the only way to fix it."

I'd been kind of thinking this same thing, all along. That maybe fighting the monsters wasn't the best way to solve the current situation. Sure, we could fight the monsters over and over again, or we could take a more active approach.

"Jason and Atty are going to get a new amphora and trap the labors again," Mia said. "That'll fix everything."

I shook my head. "That won't fix everything."

"Sure it will," Mia said. "Hera doesn't even have to be involved."

"And what?" I said. "We just go back to camp and fight these labors. Forever?"

Mia shrugged. "Sure. Camp's fun."

And Mia was crazy.

"No!" Harper said. "Logan's right. There's only one thing we can do."

"Break the curse," Daniel said.

I looked to Mom and Athena for confirmation.

They both nodded. "It's the only way," Athena said.

"So what do we do?" Harper asked.

Mom fixed her eyes on me. "You kids don't do anything."

"Are you kidding?" Mom had no idea what she was saying.

"I'm not kidding," she said. "You go back to Camp Hercules, and you stay there, safely inside the walls. Athena and I will take care of this."

I started to argue some more, but one look at Mom, and I knew there was no way she was going to change her mind. Whatever. This would not be the first time I hadn't listened to Mom.

Daughter of Zeus? That was actually pretty cool. If I'd known that when I first got to camp, I would have totally called in some favors.

"Fine," I said. "We'll go back to camp. We'll stay there."

Mia smiled, but Daniel and Harper looked like they could not believe the words had come out of my mouth. I sent them a silent message with my eyes to stay quiet.

"Great," Mom said. "I'll drive you."

But one look at Mom's car put that out of the question. The lion, in its demonic excitement, had landed on the car roof, squashing it so our car looked like it belonged in the junkyard.

"We can walk," I said.

Mom slowly shook her head, like she was trying to figure out a different way, but finally said, "Straight back to camp."

I nodded. "Straight back to camp."

Mom gave us some money and snacks.

Right before we left, Athena said, "Use it when you don't want anyone to see."

"What?" I had no clue what she was talking about. Use what?

"You'll know," Athena said. The owl on her shoulder hooted. Then she and Mom watched the four of us leave, back the way we'd come. But as soon as we were out of sight, I ducked behind the elementary school.

"We're not really going back to camp, are we?" Harper said. "Because there is no way I'm going back and hiding."

"Me either," I said. "We're going to find a way to break this curse."

**214**

 **CHAPTER 38**

We found a fast food place that the Stymphalian Birds hadn't attacked yet and got lunch with the twenty dollars Mom had insisted I take. The burger tasted like a dirty old pair of shoes, but I managed to wash it down with fries and a shake.

"We need a plan," Harper said.

Mia dipped a French fry in a giant glob of ketchup. "There is no plan. We can't just visit Hera and ask her to break some curse."

Daniel stuffed a chicken nugget in his mouth, then said something with his mouth full that sounded like, "Mia's right. Hera's really mean and will probably destroy us if we go anywhere near her."

Mia scowled at him. "Hera's not mean. She just doesn't want mortals dropping in and demanding stuff."

Harper cocked her head. "How are you such a Hera expert?"

"I'm not a Hera expert," Mia said. "I'm a mythology expert."

"So is Daniel," Harper said.

It was true. Daniel and Mia could have had a mythology trivia contest that never ended since neither of them would have gotten anything wrong.

Mia kind of smiled, but not like she really meant it. More like she had fleas and was trying not to itch. "Hera just got a bad reputation because of the whole thing with Hercules. If that was anyone's fault, it's Zeus's."

"Yeah, what about Zeus?" Harper said, looking right at me. "Can't you pull some strings with him to get us a visit with Hera?"

I'd been trying not to bring this part up, since it was still way too weird to believe.

"He doesn't live in Austin," I said.

"He lives on Mount Olympus," Daniel said.

Mom had always told me he lived near the border. I figured she meant of Mexico, not of the world of the gods. Maybe I should have asked her to be more specific.

"Still," Harper said. "You could call him."

My stomach tightened. I could not believe my grandpa was the king of the gods. "Let's just pretend I'm not related to him, okay?"

I didn't want to be related to the king of the gods. I wanted my grandpa to just be my grandpa. After this whole mess was over, Mom had some serious explaining to do. I could not believe she'd never told me anything about this.

"Okay, so Hera's mean, and isn't going to just break the curse," Harper said.

"Hera's not—" Mia started.

Harper silenced her with a look.

"What we need is to bring something to Hera that she really wants," Harper said. "Then we can make a deal. We give it to her if she agrees to break the curse."

Mia laughed, but Daniel's eyes got super wide.

"That's a great idea," he said. "The gods and goddesses love stuff. Like sacrifices. And gifts. That's perfect. You're really smart, Harper."

"I know," Harper said, eating a fry.

"What does Hera want?" I asked. "Like if I were a god and had crazy awesome powers, what would I need that people like us could give me?"

Harper put her hand to her mouth as she thought, but Daniel snapped his fingers.

"The apples!" he said.

"Atty's apples?" I asked.

"Exactly! You see, there was this contest where Discord tossed this golden apple into a wedding where Hera, Athena, and Aphrodite fought over it. And Aphrodite got it. Hera never got over that. It's one of the reasons she's so mean. If we could bring her Atty's apples—or even just one of them—I bet you she would totally break the curse."

I thought it through and tried to find something wrong with it, but I'd seen those golden apples. I wasn't even a goddess, and I wanted them.

"That's a really great idea," I said.

Harper stood and threw her tray away. "So we head back to camp and get the apples."

I stood also. "Yep. Then we go to Mount Olympus and make our deal."

We managed to avoid any monsters on our way back to Camp Hercules, but Austin itself wasn't having the same luck. It was a good thing Mom hadn't driven us. Traffic was backed up for miles and didn't look like it was moving. Walking was way faster. Pretty soon we saw the shiny walls of Camp Hercules ahead.

They'd managed to shut the gate. Hercules was nowhere to be seen. Jason and Atty also weren't around. I guess they'd gone off to try to get a new amphora. But Achilles, Odysseus, Cassie, and Helen were there, standing guard on top of the fence.

"Hey!" I said, waving. "We decided to come back."

Achilles glared at us, like he had no idea who we were. Not like it wasn't obvious. We had our camp T-shirts on, not to mention we'd talked to him lots of times before.

"Are you spies?" Helen asked, frowning down at us. She even looked pretty when she was frowning.

Harper stepped forward. "We're not spies. We're campers. You know us."

Achilles nodded slowly. "I know you. But I also know you were sent out to fight the labors. Why are you back?"

I glanced to Harper, who gave a small shake of her head. It was way better to keep our plan quiet, especially since there might be a spy for Hera somewhere at camp.

"We forgot something?" I said.

It was a totally lame excuse, and they didn't buy it for a second.

"Then you don't need it," Odysseus said. "Everyone has a job. You kids need to go back to fighting monsters."

I tried to think of something else to convince them, because we really needed to get in there to get the apples, but then Daniel said, under his breath, "I have another idea."

Daniel might not be the bravest guy, but he was smart. He knew what he was talking about. I stepped back. "Okay, fine, we'll go back to fighting monsters, risking our lives, you know, just the usual."

"Good!" Achilles said.

And that was the end of that conversation. The gate stayed closed, and we walked away.

"What's your plan?" I asked Daniel.

He took off his glasses to clean them, because they were covered with dirt, then shoved them back on, crooked. "The apples," he said.

"Are inside camp," I said. "Which was why we needed to go in there."

He shook his head. "There are other apples."

"Oh yeah!" Mia said, and I felt like I was caught in the middle of their mythology trivia contest with no clue what they were talking about.

"What other apples?" I said.

"The labors," Daniel said. "Remember Team Apple?"

I scanned through what little I knew of all the labors. I'd been so focused on the Hydra that I'd forgotten most of them. But that's right. There was some bunk that had to pick apples for their labor.

"Are those golden apples?" I asked.

Daniel almost jumped up and down with excitement. "They're totally golden apples. And even better, those apples—"

Mia's face fell. "Oh yeah. They're the ones that Hera gave to Zeus as a wedding present. We can't take those. If we steal those apples, it would be really disrespectful to Hera."

"Who cares?" I said. "It just means that if we steal those apples, she'll want them even more. And maybe Hera doesn't deserve that much respect."

Mia frowned. But I didn't care. This was even better than Atty's apples. Us not getting into camp was actually really lucky.

"This isn't a good idea," Mia said, but we all ignored her.

"So where do we find these apples?" Harper asked. "Do you think they're inside camp?"

Daniel glanced back in the direction of Camp Hercules. If they were inside, that wouldn't help us much.

"No, since they're a labor, there's a really good chance they're gone," Daniel said. "But there is one way to find out for sure."

"Great," I said. "How?" I loved when things were for sure. For sure meant easy.

Daniel shrugged. "We have to find and capture a shape-shifting god. Then we have to make him tell us."

Maybe it wasn't going to be so easy after all.

# CHAPTER 39

"T"he location of the Apples of Hesperides is completely secret," Daniel said.

I waited. There had to be more to what he was saying, otherwise we were doomed to failure before we even started.

"But," Daniel said, "If we talk to this shapeshifting sea god, the Old Man of the Sea, he'll tell us where the apples are."

"That's all we have to do?" I said. "Talk to some old guy who tells us where the golden apples are? We can totally do that." He'd made it sound impossible before.

Mia scuffed her feet on the ground. "I don't like this idea at all. I don't think we should do it."

We all three looked at her like she was crazy.

"What do you suggest then? Just fight the Hydra over

and over again until finally we get sick of it and the monster kills us?" Harper said.

"No, of course not," Mia said. "But I don't think we should steal these apples. It's wrong. And it's not our labor. I'm not going to do it."

"Then don't," Harper said.

"Fine, I won't."

They glared at each other, like they were having a staring contest, and finally Mia stepped back. "You know what? I'll catch you guys later. I have things I need to do."

And without another word, she turned and walked away.

"Well that was weird," I said. Mia was acting really strange. I mean sure, she was a total rule follower, and we'd had to nearly twist her arm to get her to cover for us when we'd freed Prometheus. But why would she care so much about stealing the apples? We were going to save Camp Hercules. We were going to break the curse.

"Do you think she'll come back?" Daniel asked, watching her go.

Harper sniffed. "Yeah, maybe. She's probably going to go off and pout for a while, but then she'll come back. Anyway, back to the plan. Where's this Old Man of the Sea?"

Daniel's eyes got wide again. He was back in his element. "Right. He's the sea god, Nereus. He guards the location of the Garden of the Hesperides where the golden apples grow."

"And we find him where?" I said.

"Hmmm . . . ," Daniel said. "He's probably near water. But you know Austin. There's always a drought. This summer isn't any different. So it would have to be a lot of water. And somewhere where he could blend in. He doesn't like to be noticed."

"There's the lake downtown," I said. Mom took me jogging on weekends sometimes. It would be the perfect place to blend in. There were always tons of people around, and there was lots of water, even during the driest of summers.

Daniel seemed to consider this, then nodded. "Yeah, that's a great idea. That's part of the river. And if he's in the river, then he's kind of able to be everywhere the water connects at once."

"How does that work?" I asked.

Harper smacked me. "He's a god, Logan. Gods can do things, remember?"

It was like I always wanted to forget this. The gods and their powers were a little overwhelming at times.

We managed to catch a bus with our leftover change, and since there was a dedicated bus lane, even with the traffic, we made it downtown in record time. We got off and walked the rest of the way to Town Lake.

"Isn't that Ani?" Harper said, pointing at a kid sitting on a bench by the water. He wore a green T-shirt and matching green bandana.

"Who?" I asked. With the shirt and bandana, he had to be part of Camp Hercules.

Harper started over for him, so Daniel and I followed. "Ani," she said. "He's on Team Apple."

"No way," Daniel said. "Maybe he can just tell us where the garden is."

"Or we can just ask the sea god ourselves and not get

anyone else involved," I said. Since we weren't exactly following camp rules, I figured it would be better the fewer people that knew our plan.

"I don't know," Daniel said. "I think the more help we can get, the better."

"Hey, Ani!" Harper said.

Ani whipped around and had a look on his face like he'd been caught stealing all the cookies from the pantry.

"What are you guys doing here?" Ani said. He was short, like maybe one of the shortest kids in camp, and had super thick dark hair that looked like he'd never brushed it since camp had started.

"What are you doing here?" I asked quickly. Maybe he'd just leave and we could get on with our plan.

Harper didn't seem to have the same concerns as me. She smiled and said, "We're trying to find the Garden of the Hesperides. You don't happen to know where it is, do you?"

Ani blew out a long breath. "I wish. But Nereus won't talk to me. He says that he doesn't want Team Apple to know."

"So it is out of camp?" Daniel said. "Right?"

"Yeah, right," Ani said. "I went to check on it, you know, after the gate got opened, because I was going to try to stop it, but somehow the entire thing was gone. Trees, nymphs, dragon . . . everything."

"Dragon?" I shot a look at Daniel who kind of grinned and cowered.

"Yeah, you know," Ani said. "The dragon that guards the apples. He has a hundred heads."

"A hundred heads?" I was sounding a little like a parrot,

but at this point, I didn't care. "You're telling me that in addition to finding this garden, we have to fight a dragon to get the apples?"

"Well, yeah," Ani said. "And that's if you can get by the crazy, blood-sucking nymphs."

This was getting worse by the second.

"It sounds impossible," Harper said. "How did you guys do it?" By the tone of her voice, I knew she was prying. It was the same voice she used when we were in the Underworld and she was trying to get information from Charon.

Ani shook his head. "We haven't yet. All we managed to do back at camp was find out where the garden was. But now, since Nereus won't talk to me, I can't even get that far."

Maybe this sea god wouldn't talk to Ani, but he would talk to me. I was Zeus' grandson after all.

"Where is he?" I asked.

Ani pointed to a taco stand near the bank of the river. "He's been eating tacos for the last two hours. They're having some kind of special."

Four people sat at the taco stand. Two of them looked like college kids, one looked like she was someone's mom, and the other was an old guy with stringy gray hair that had little bits of green stuff tangled into it. Maybe seaweed. That had to be Nereus.

I walked to the taco stand. "Hey, Nereus, can I talk to you for a minute?"

I didn't think anything would happen, with as pessimistic as Ani was being, but the old guy whipped his head around and looked directly at me.

"Hey!" I said, waving. "I'm Logan. You know, from Camp Hercules." This was going better than I had thought.

Except then Nereus grumbled something under his breath and turned back to the taco stand.

"I told you so," Ani said when I walked back to them.

"So what do we do?" Harper asked. "How do we get him to talk to us?"

"Well, when Hercules did this, he grabbed hold of him and didn't let him go until Nereus told him where the garden was," Daniel said. "So that's what we need to do."

Ani laughed. "Yeah, go ahead and try."

That sounded easy enough. I walked up to him again and said his name. He turned around to face me, just like before. I immediately jumped for him, arms out, and grabbed him. Or at least I tried to grab him. But as my hands came together, there was nothing in them. Then water covered my head and I was gasping for air.

Water? That made no sense. I swam to the surface. Somehow I was in the middle of the lake, far from the taco stand. Nereus was still back at the taco stand, not even looking at me.

I swam back to shore. Both Harper and Daniel were trying not to laugh.

"How did that happen?" I said. "How are we supposed to catch him? That's not even possible."

"He's a god, Logan," Harper said.

"Well, when Hercules did it . . . ," Daniel started, but his words started fading away and my mind went a little fuzzy. From somewhere nearby, an owl hooted. Then in the back of my mind, I heard Athena's voice. *Use it when you don't want anyone to see.* I'd had no clue what she was talking about before, but now it made perfect sense.

My fingers went to the thin golden crown under my shirt, tucked into the waist of my shorts. I hadn't tried on the crown on yet, but I knew this is what Athena was talking about. The owl hooted again.

"I have a plan," I said, cutting off Daniel mid-sentence. I wasn't sure what he was saying, but he didn't seem to mind.

"What?" Harper said.

"I'll tell you after it works."

I walked toward the taco stand again, but this time, before I got to him, I pulled the crown out and put it on. Something must've happened, because from behind me, Daniel said, "No way. That is awesome!"

I looked down at my arm but couldn't see it. The crown made me invisible!

"Hey, Nereus," I said.

He turned around, and I immediately jumped forward. This time I connected. I wrapped both arms around him and interlaced my fingers.

"Show yourself, coward!" the sea god yelled as he twisted around.

This was perfect! The crown had made me invisible. But now that I had him, I wasn't sure what I was supposed to do.

# CHAPTER 40

Nereus twisted around in my arms, but I held on as tightly as I could. Then he turned into a lion and tried to claw at me, but since I was holding him from the side, his claws couldn't reach me. Then he turned into a bear.

"What's happening?" I shouted.

"He's shapeshifting," Daniel said. "Just keep holding on. He'll stop soon."

Oh yeah. I forgot about the shapeshifting thing. With these claws he'd probably tear me to shreds before I even had a chance to let go. But I kept holding on. He turned into a snake next, then a turtle. Then he turned into Athena, and I felt really bad grabbing hold of her, but it wasn't really her. It was the same grouchy sea god, and I knew that if I let go now, I would never get another chance. So I held on.

Nereus went through twenty more transformations, even turning into an armadillo. I did not let go, and finally he shifted back into the grumpy old man he'd started as.

"Let me go," he snarled.

I did not let him go. "Not until you tell us what we need to know."

"What you need to know?" Nereus said. "What you need to know is some manners. Grabbing onto me. What do you think you're doing? Don't you know I'm a god?"

"That's what I've heard," I said. "But you're the only one who can help us save Camp Hercules."

Nereus laughed. "Save Camp Hercules? Why should I help with that? I sure don't want to be trapped inside those walls again. Not a taco stand for miles. And if those cattle got any closer to the banks of the river, I was going to die from the odor. Have you smelled them?"

Just hearing about the cattle made the memories come back. "Yeah, I've smelled them," I said. "It's not that bad."

Nereus struggled against me. "Well the taco part is. So I'm not helping."

This was not going the way I hoped. Sure, at least we were now having a conversation, but it was going nowhere fast.

"I know how to make tacos," Daniel said. "I learned at our global festival at school last year. I could open a taco stand when we get back."

Nereus craned his neck around to look at Daniel. "A real taco stand? With corn tortillas, not that flour imitation stuff?"

"Totally," Daniel said. "Only corn. And you won't ever

have to pay."

"Well, I should hope not," Nereus said. He was still trying to act tough, but was softening as the seconds went by.

"Could you add French fries to the taco stand?" Ani asked.

"No French fries," Daniel said. "Just tacos. And I'll name the taco stand Nereus Tacos."

That was like the icing on the cake. Nereus actually smiled.

"Let me guess," Nereus said. "You want to know where the Garden of the Hesperides is."

I did not loosen my grip. I was guessing I was still invisible since I had the crown on, but I didn't risk letting go. He could still be tricking us.

"Exactly," Harper said. "Then Logan will let you go."

"Logan . . . ," Nereus said. "I'll remember that."

That was perfect.

"But you can't tell the kid from Team Apple," Nereus said. "That would be too easy for him."

"Oh, come on," Ani said. "I'm the one who tracked you here."

"Even more the reason," Nereus said. "Now you'll have to track me again."

It didn't bother me if Ani knew or not. "Fine. We won't tell him."

But Nereus set his face and said, "Once he's gone, I'll tell you."

Ani complained a little bit longer, but I really wished he'd stop because it wasn't easy to keep holding onto the sea god.

Finally Ani scowled and wandered far enough away that he couldn't hear.

"That's good," Nereus said. "Okay, the garden is about a mile north of Camp Hercules. It's tucked away in Northside Park. Go to the back of the park. Turn left at the purple picnic table. Then you'll find it."

Northside Park. Purple picnic table. I looked to Harper and Daniel, but they couldn't tell since I was still invisible. So I said, "Should I let him go now?"

"Yes, I told you what you needed to know," Nereus said, shrugging against me. "You don't want to get any more on my bad side than you already have, do you?"

I didn't.

"Totally trust him," Daniel said. "I'm pretty sure he can't lie about the location."

That worked for me. My arms were aching from holding on for so long. I let go and stepped back, taking the crown off and tucking it away before anyone could get a good look at it.

Nereus whipped around to face me. "You know that Hades has a crown that makes him invisible."

Did I look like I would know that? He had me confused with Daniel.

"That's interesting." I hoped he wouldn't run around telling any of the other gods that I had the crown since it might get back to Hephaestus that I'd stolen it.

"If I were you, I'd keep it secret," Nereus said. "Otherwise one of the gods might try to steal it from you."

"Thanks for the advice," I said. As if I didn't already

have enough to worry about.

Nereus pointed a finger at Daniel. "If I get sent back to Camp Hercules, I'm holding you to that taco stand thing. And if you don't deliver, I'm feeding you to the dragon."

Daniel looked like he wanted to pee his pants, but he only nodded. Then Nereus turned his back on us and sauntered to the taco stand.

Daniel slapped me on the back. "Dude, you are totally like Hades! That's awesome."

Harper didn't look nearly so excited. "Bet you stole that from Hephaestus, didn't you?"

"Maybe," I said.

"You know that's going to be trouble, right?"

Everything was trouble. I figured it was just one more thing to add to the growing list.

"We should head north," I said.

We still had to get the apples. But at least this sea god stuff was behind us. That had to be the worst part.

# CHAPTER 41

Ani begged me to tell him what Nereus had said. He started naming off the reasons why we had to take him along, stating why it was impossible to get the apples.

"We got this covered," I said. "Don't you realize that the three of us are part of Team Hydra? We fought the Hydra. Like the actual, real-life Hydra. It had nine heads."

"Thirteen," Daniel said. "If you count the ones that grew back."

"I totally count those. Nothing is worse than the Hydra."

But Ani shook his head. "The Hydra is easy. It's like child's play. You need me."

I didn't say a word. I was going to keep my promise.

Finally Ani stomped off and sat back down on the bench by the water. As far as I was concerned, he and the rest of the kids on Team Apple had it easy. We didn't owe him anything.

Harper, Daniel, and I hopped back on the bus and headed north. We were just passing the Capitol when Harper elbowed me in the side.

"Look over there," she said, pointing.

We all turned to look. There, on the front steps and lawn of the Capitol building, were at least a hundred Amazon women on horses with bows and arrows and swords and shields. It didn't look like anyone was fighting, but they also weren't waving a flag of surrender.

"Yikes," Daniel said. "They're going to take over the entire city."

"Or the world," Harper said. But she said it almost like she admired them. Like she wanted to be one of them.

"Is that Mia?" Daniel said.

He pointed, but by the time I looked, the bus had gone too far by to see.

"Why would Mia be hanging out with the Amazons?" I asked.

"Because they're awesome," Harper said. "If I wasn't here with you guys, I would totally join the Amazons."

"Good to know," I said.

The bus let us off about half a block from the park.

The park was like a mishmash of people eating lunch, walking dogs, and taking selfies. We hurried through, looking for the purple picnic table. We finally found it, buried in the thickest part of the trees. Then we turned left.

"You really think there's a dragon?" I asked as we ducked between branches. As far as I could see, there were only normal trees. No trees with golden apples and no mythological creatures.

"That's what the myths all say," Daniel whispered.

"And do they say how to defeat this dragon?" I wasn't sure the invisibility trick would work again. I also didn't want to grab hold of a scaly dragon that might breathe fire and incinerate me on the spot.

"Not really," Daniel said. "The myths just say that Hercules defeated him."

I shrugged. "So maybe he's easy to defeat." That had to be it. If it wasn't even worth a footnote to talk about the battle between Hercules and this dragon, then how hard could it be?

"Guys, I don't think so," Harper said. She came to a stop at the edge of a clearing. In the center of the clearing stood a single tree. Plump golden apples hung from its branches. Apples just like the ones Atty had.

The second I saw them, I knew I had to have the apples, no matter what. But curled around the tree trunk was the hugest dragon that I'd ever seen. Okay, fine, it was the only dragon I'd ever seen, but it was still pretty wicked.

"That's him," Daniel said.

At the sound of his voice, the eyes on the creature opened. When I say that it was a dragon, it might have been more accurate to say that it was an impossibly big snake with one hundred heads, each the size of a cantaloupe. Each head had two eyes, which meant two-hundred eyes looked our way. Then one hundred tongues flicked out, like they were all tasting us to see if we were worthy of being their appetizer.

"How do we fight that?" I whispered. Not that it mattered if I kept my voice down now.

One of the heads immediately darted out. We jumped back, and its fangs narrowly missed my arm.

"How does it reach that far?" I yelled.

Daniel pulled his sword from his belt and swiped at the head. He didn't even come close. Worse, he dropped his sword.

"Uh, can you get that for me, Logan?" he asked.

"Are you kidding me?" I said. "You want me to die instead of you? Let me guess. The venom is poisonous."

"Totally," Harper said. "I heard that some girl on Team Apple had to get rushed to the nurse for a special antidote."

"There's a nurse at Camp Hercules?" Daniel said. "How

did I not know that?"

He was right. Jason and Atty had never mentioned anything about a nurse. But then again, when I'd almost died from Hydra poisoning, they'd used the Golden Fleece to heal me.

"Maybe they figured Team Hydra doesn't need a nurse because we're too epic," Harper said.

I almost gave her a high-five, but since we were about to die from the hideous snake dragon, I figured maybe it wasn't the time.

"Did the girl live?" Daniel asked.

"I don't know," Harper said. Which might as well have been no.

"So we can't get near it," I said. "Then we'll use our spears."

I grabbed my spear from off my back, and it immediately grew until it was seven feet long. I spun it around in front of me, held my shield securely with my other arm, then pulled back and threw. I aimed perfectly. There was no way I could miss. But the dragon thing twisted its body, missing the spear, then lash out with two more of its heads. Since I was almost leaning forward, I felt the tongues on my face.

"You missed," Harper said.

I wiped at my face to get the dragon grossness off. What if its tongue was poison? I could die right here, right now.

"Thanks for pointing that out," I said. "Do you have any ideas?"

Harper smiled. "Maybe we're not using the right weapon."

I was sure she was going to pull out her circle-thing and throw it at the dragon. There was no way she'd have better luck with that. But instead, she reached into her back pocket and pulled out one of the red feathers.

"The Stymphalian Bird!" Daniel said. "It's a natural enemy of snakes."

"Exactly," Harper said, then she threw the feather, pointy end first, toward the dragon/snake.

Her throw was nowhere near hard enough, and her aim wasn't even good, but the feather picked up speed as it went almost like the bird that it had come from was controlling it.

The hundred heads of the snake darted around the feather, keeping away from it while also trying to knock it off its course. But the feather moved like a remote control airplane, traveling any way it needed to reach its victim. When it finally reached the tree, it burrowed into the body of the dragon and stayed there. Then the dragon fell to the ground and sank into the earth, just like the Nemean Lion had done earlier today.

"You got it!" Daniel said. "You think it's going back to Camp Hercules to regenerate? Or will it regenerate here?"

"Not our problem," I said. I took a step for the tree, but right then, three women materialized in front of it. They were green and covered in bark and leaves, and when they smiled, they exposed huge fangs so white the sun reflected off them.

"Who killed our dragon?" one of them hissed.

We were in serious trouble.

# CHAPTER 42

"Come closer and die," one of the women said.

With the saliva dripping from their fangs, I didn't doubt them for a second. They made the Fates look like a knitting club.

"How are we supposed to get by them?" I said, taking a step back from the vampire nymphs. I could almost imagine them sinking their fangs into my neck and sucking every drop of blood from my body. "What did Hercules do?" Harper only had one more feather, and there were three of these demon women protecting the tree.

"Well," Daniel started. "There are a few different theories on that . . ."

"No theories! What do we do?" I couldn't reach my spear, but I grabbed my sword.

Harper leaned over and whispered. "Use your invisibility."

That would have been great, except they were all staring right at me. It wasn't like I could take them by surprise. Not with those fangs.

"Too late," I said. "We need a different plan." If they were some kind of mythological vampires, they sure weren't acting like normal vampires that I'd read about. Normally vampires hated the sun, but here they were, in broad daylight having no issues at all.

"Hercules got Atlas to get the apples for him," Daniel said. "Because Atlas is their dad or something like that."

That was something. "Where do we find Atlas?" I'd heard his name before, but that was about it.

"You don't," Daniel said. "He's the Titan who holds up the world. And the only way Hercules got him to do it was to hold the world in his place."

Hold the world? How was that even possible? But something about his words tickled my brain. "What do you mean Titan?"

Daniel's eyes got really wide. "Atlas is a Titan, but he's not the only one."

"Prometheus!" Harper said.

We not only knew a Titan, he owed us a favor.

I stepped back, away from the vampire nymphs. "We call Prometheus, he gets the apples, and then we go see Hera. Sound good?"

"Sounds excellent," Harper said.

"Except you can never trust the Titans," Daniel added.

Whatever. I wasn't going to worry about that right now. I lifted my head and said, "Hey, Prometheus, if you can hear us, we want to call in our favor."

Nothing happened. So I said it again. I don't know what I was expecting—maybe giant footsteps coming our way as the Titan got closer—but that wasn't what happened. What did happen was that after the tenth time I called on Prometheus, something flew at us really fast, so fast that I couldn't see what it was until it landed five feet in front of us.

It wasn't a bird. It definitely wasn't Prometheus. It was a grungy-looking teenager with crazy curly hair. He wore red clothes, and on top of his head was some kind of hat that made it look like he had wings growing out the sides of his head.

Wait! He did have wings growing out of the sides of his head!

"Hermes?" Daniel said, then he looked at me quickly. "He's the messenger god."

Daniel was getting better at realizing I didn't know anything.

"Messenger god?" I said. "Does that mean you have a message?"

"Oh yeah," Hermes said, tipping his hat at us in some kind of greeting. The wings stayed in place. "I have three messages. The first message is from Prometheus."

Perfect!

"He says that if you call his name one more time he's going to accidentally step on you," Hermes said.

Okay, so that wasn't the best news.

"But he owes us a favor," I said. I tried not to sound like a whiny brat, but seriously? We'd saved Prometheus from having his liver eaten every single day by two giant eagles.

Hermes put up his hand. "Yeah, yeah, just hold on."

"What's the second message?" Harper said.

Hermes grinned. "Right. You'll love this one. It's from Logan's mom and Athena."

A hard ball formed in my stomach. Uh oh.

"They say that you need to stop what you're doing right now," Hermes said. "You mom says that you are going to be grounded for the next year if you don't listen to her."

"Grounded for a year! Are you kidding me?"

"What can I say?" Hermes said. "She and Athena told me that you kids aren't supposed to be anywhere near here, and you certainly aren't supposed to be trying to get apples to bribe Hera."

At his words, thunder rumbled in the distance. It had to be some weird coincidence.

"What are you going to do, Logan?" Daniel asked.

What? Did he expect me to just give up now? We had to do this. We had to break the curse, and I figured we had a better chance of it than anyone else. I wasn't sure why I felt this way. It was just this feeling I had, like I was sure we were the only hope for Camp Hercules.

"Nothing," I said. "I'm sure she's not serious."

"Oh, she's serious," Hermes said. "The only reason she's not here herself is because she and Athena are trapped at the zoo."

"Trapped at the zoo? Why?"

Hermes put up his hands. "Don't worry about it. I'll take care of that later."

"What about the third message?" Harper said.

"Right, the third message. That's also from Prometheus. He says for you kids to meet him by the fountain at the front of the park."

Now that was good news. "So he's going to help us," I said.

"I don't know what he's going to do," Hermes said. "All I do is deliver the messages."

And without another word, Hermes lifted into the air and flew off in a blur.

"Come closer," the vampire nymphs called, reaching their hands out for us.

If we didn't have to get any closer to them ever, that would be awesome. "Maybe later," I said. "Come on, you guys. Let's go find the Titan."

# CHAPTER 43

We ran to the fountain by the front of the park. There was no sign of Prometheus.

"Do you think he meant right now?" Harper asked.

"I guess so," I said. I hoped he didn't mean next week. We needed to break this curse right away.

"Maybe this isn't a good idea," Daniel said, but his words were drowned out as giant booming sounds started approaching, like footsteps.

The water of the fountain shook with each one, making ripples. There were maybe five other people around, and they all jumped to their feet. Then the Titan came into view.

Prometheus was even bigger than the last time we'd seen him. He wore real clothes also which was an improvement because his other clothes had been torn to rags. Each step he took covered almost an entire block, and when the people around the fountain saw him, they took off running.

Okay, that's not completely true. A couple of them started filming him on their phones, but then they chickened out and ran. Still, those videos would go viral on the Internet.

By the time Prometheus got to the fountain, there was nobody else around but the three of us.

"Hey, kid," Prometheus said. "I heard you the first time you called." He didn't sound nearly as appreciative as he had when we rescued him from the side of the mountain.

"How was I supposed to know that?" I said. It wasn't like I was some expert in dealing with the Greek gods.

Prometheus scowled. "Because I told you that all you had to do was call me, and I'd come. Did you think I wasn't good for my word?"

At this last part he leaned close, making it obvious that I looked like an ant compared to this guy.

"I'd never think that," I said, trying not to back away from him. But he was seriously intimidating.

That was when I noticed that he had my bandana tied around his wrist. But it didn't seem like the best time to ask for it, so I bit my tongue.

"What do you need?" Prometheus asked, eyeing each of us.

"Oh, right," I said. "We need a few of the apples of the Hesperides. But they're really scary and we can't get past them."

"Of course they're scary," Prometheus said. "They're supposed to be scary. That's because no one is supposed to take the apples." He crossed his giant arms which made it seem like that was the end of that conversation.

"They're doing a really great job," Daniel said. "Do they suck blood like vampires, because that's what we thought?"

At this, Prometheus put back his head and laughed. "Of course they suck blood. How do you think vampire rumors got started?"

"Count Dracula?" Daniel said. "Legend has it that he started as Vlad—"

Prometheus cocked his head. "Is this relevant?"

Daniel cleared his throat and stopped talking. "I guess not."

I hated to get right to the point, but pretty soon news crews would be here filming everything. Once this curse was broken, the gods were going to have a lot of covering up to do.

"We want to call in our favor," I said. "We want you to get us a few of the apples."

Prometheus put a finger to his lips, like he was considering this. "That's a pretty big favor."

It didn't seem that big to me. All he had to do was walk over and pluck some apples from the tree. He couldn't possibly be scared of the nymphs.

"True," I said. "But you did make a promise."

"Yeah, you're right, kid," Prometheus said. "And I'm not gonna go back on my word."

"Awesome! Thank you."

"But . . . ," Prometheus started.

Here it came. There was always some catch.

"I'll get the apples," Prometheus said. "But after I do, you have to get me the key for the Olympian gods' palace."

I nodded even though I had no idea what he was talking about.

"Where do we get that?" Harper asked.

Prometheus pointed in the direction of Camp Hercules. We weren't too far away, but still couldn't see Mount Olympus. "I traveled to the top of Mount Olympus to speak to Zeus, but the doors to the palace were locked. Then, when I knocked politely, they wouldn't let me in. I'm not going to knock again. That's where you kids come in. You have to promise me you'll get the key. It's in a cave, guarded by the Sphinx. You can't miss it."

Stealing a key to the home of the gods didn't sound like a good idea, even to me. But it wasn't like we had much choice.

"We can't—" Daniel started.

I cut him off. If we had a key, we could sneak in when we got there and take Hera by surprise. "We'll get you the key," I said. And since things were going so well, I decided to push my luck. "Can I have my bandana back also?"

"No," Prometheus said, then he walked away, heading back to the tree with the golden apples, deep in the park.

"We can't get him the key," Daniel said.

I fixed my eyes on him. "Do you have a better plan?"

"No. But you have no idea what we're up against."

"We just defeated a dragon. How much worse can it be?" I said.

"I'm just saying you made him another promise," Daniel said. "The first one already got us in enough trouble. Now you want to steal a key that you definitely shouldn't steal. But if you don't deliver, you're going to have an angry Titan on your hands."

Everything Daniel said was true, but it didn't make a difference.

Prometheus returned about half hour later and squatted down to our level. He held our missing weapons and one golden apple. I was pretty sure I'd asked for three apples, and I almost said something, but a really smart part of my brain told me this wasn't the best idea. One would have to do. I wanted to grab the apple from his hands, but I managed enough self-control not to do it.

"It took you longer than I would have thought," I said.

Daniel smacked me. But come on. All he had to do was grab the apple off the tree and walk away.

"I had lunch with the Hesperides," Prometheus said, handing my spear back to me. He also gave Daniel his sword.

"Lunch!" With vampire nymphs? Better him than us, seeing as how we would have been on the menu.

"Well, sure. It would have been rude to just grab the apple and leave. And they made golden apple turnovers with hot icing on top. Best I've had in centuries." He held the apple out. "Remember our deal, right?"

"The key. We are on it," I said.

Prometheus handed the apple over. Warm fuzziness moved through my body, contentment like I'd never felt before in my life. Everything was going to work out perfectly. I knew it. We had the apple, and nothing was going to go wrong.

# CHAPTER 44

"Let me see it," Harper said. She reached for the apple, like she wanted to hold it, but I pulled it back.

"I'll hold it," I said.

"I just want to see it."

Did she? What if she wanted to steal it? What if she never gave it back? Or what about Daniel? He could take it and run away with it.

Okay, these were crazy thoughts, and I knew that, but I couldn't get them out of my mind. I shook my head, as if maybe that would somehow dislodge the thoughts.

Harper held her hand out and waited, frowning at me the entire time. It took every bit of effort I had, but I finally managed to give her the apple. The second it was out of my hand, I wanted it back.

She turned it around and looked at it, and her eyes got

a little glazed over. "Oh, now I get it," she said. Her fingers tightened.

"Yeah," I said. "It's hard to let go of."

"Well, I don't have any intention of holding it," Daniel said. "And that's just great if you guys want to stay here all day and pass it back and forth, but it's getting dark. We need to get back to camp."

I glanced up. He was right. The sun was actually close to setting. If we didn't figure something out, we'd be sleeping here at the park until morning.

I grabbed the apple back from Harper.

"Hey!" she said, but I ignored her.

"We need to get back to camp," I said, and we set off, in the direction of Camp Hercules.

It wasn't far away, and before long, we came to the shiny golden fence that surrounded the entire camp. We were somewhere around back, with the gate nowhere close to us. But before we'd walked for even a minute, we rounded a bend, and stopped.

The three Fates stood in our path. They wore their usual clothes, black pants and colored tank tops, one red, one blue, and one yellow. The bright colored matching streaks in their spiky gray hair looked like it had been freshly touched up with spray paint.

"Hey, Sugar Plum, looks like you need to get into camp," the Fate on the left, in the red shirt, said. She held the iPad of Doom and tapped it with her long finger.

"Uh, yeah," I said.

"We're heading to the gate," Daniel said. "They'll let

us in."

"They won't let you in," the Fate on the right, in the blue shirt, said. "They'll make you sleep out here with the monsters." She held giant scissors and opened and closed them, like she was marking off the beat to a rap song.

"We've seen the future," the Fate in the middle said. "The monsters will close in on you."

Daniel shuddered at this last part, like he almost felt the monsters around him.

"We never did talk about how we'd get them to open the gate," Harper said. "We can't exactly tell them our plan. One of them could be the spy."

It was a really valid point, and I knew exactly where this whole encounter with the Fates was going. They weren't here by chance. Nothing the Fates did was just lucky coincidence.

I crossed my arms, still holding the golden apple. I was not letting the thing go. "Fine," I said. "How much to get us into camp?" In my mind, I went over what the maximum amount I was willing to part with was. Maybe ten minutes. Fifteen if I had to negotiate.

"Ten years," the Fate on the left said.

I choked on my saliva. "Ten years! Are you kidding?" I couldn't give up ten years of my life. Sure, I had to save the world, but ten years was a lot of time. Even split between the three of us, that was still over three years per person. If the Fates wouldn't let us in, we'd have to try our luck at the front gate.

"Do we have a deal?" the Fate in the middle said. She held a giant ball of yarn and started pulling on the end of it.

"No! We don't have a deal." I was not giving up ten years of my life.

But just then, Mia ran up, from who knows where. "Don't do it," Mia said. "Just forget about the whole thing. They're trying to trick you."

Of course the Fates were trying to trick us. Every single mythology thing we'd met was not what it seemed to be. But Prometheus had been willing to negotiate. Maybe the Fates would be also.

"What about five years?" I said. It was way longer that I wanted, but I couldn't offer up a day at this point and hope they'd agree.

"No deal," the Fate with the scissors said. "Ten years or nothing, Dumpling."

I noticed Harper and Daniel had been especially quiet this entire time, like they didn't want to get caught in the middle of some bartering for time off their lives.

"Two years," I said. I wasn't thinking straight.

"No again," the Fate with the iPad said.

Think. I had to think. Maybe . . .

"What about a bargain?" I said.

The Fate in the middle lowered the ball of yarn. "What kind of bargain, Sweet Pea?"

I'd already made one great bargain today. Another one couldn't hurt.

"How about if you get us into Camp Hercules, we'll owe you a favor?" I said.

All three Fates cocked their heads, as if they were considering a proposition they'd never considered before.

"What kind of favor, Darling?" the Fate with the scissors said.

I had no idea what kind of favor the Fates would need. Maybe they needed someone to color their hair. Or sweep around the Trading Post.

"What do you want?" I said. "Name it and we'll do it."

Harper smacked me. "Are you sure about that, Logan?" she whispered.

"Just walk away," Mia said, almost pulling on my arm.

What was it with them? They both knew we had to do this.

"We've seen the future," the Fate with the iPad said. She held up the screen almost like she was going to show us the future, but the only thing I saw on the iPad was the giant eyeball.

"The future is not bright," the Fate with the yarn said.

"But with your help, we could change the future," the Fate with the scissors said.

I forced a smile onto my face, like that sounded great to me. But seriously, the Fates wanted us to help them change the future? Still, if it would get us into camp . . .

"How?" I said.

"There is a way," the Fate with the iPad said.

"Help us capture the Titan," the Fate with the yarn said. "That is the favor."

Next to me, Daniel started coughing, like he was choking.

"You want us to help you capture a Titan?" I said. Like Prometheus? But we'd just freed him.

"That is the favor," the Fate with the scissors said. "Do

you kids accept it?"

She seemed to say, '*You better accept it or you will die.*' But still, capturing a Titan seemed like a pretty big job. Maybe there was a way to agree without really committing.

"We'll do our best," I said. There, that was good. I hadn't said that we would actually do it. And I hadn't said that we wouldn't.

"Then it's a deal," the Fate with the iPad said. She held out the iPad. I touched the eyeball on the screen, which lit up green.

It was a deal, whether I wanted it to be or not.

The giant golden wall of Camp Hercules seemed to tear itself apart, brick by brick, and rebuild itself around us, making sure we were on the inside. When it finished rebuilding, the Fates were nowhere to be seen. I had this really bad feeling that I had somehow sealed my doom. I now owed a favor not only to Prometheus, but also to the Fates, and too bad for me, both of them were linked together.

I was in serious trouble, and we hadn't even come close to finishing our job.

# CHAPTER 45

"This is a really bad idea," Mia said the second the wall closed behind us.

"No way!" Daniel said. "Did you see that? That was the coolest thing ever! And you know the best part?"

We were inside the wall and that much closer to breaking the curse. That was the best part as far as I was concerned.

"What?" Harper said.

"The monsters!" Daniel said. "They're all outside the wall."

Almost like it was mocking him, the ground started rumbling, like thunder coming from underground. We ducked behind the nearest trees, even though they couldn't possibly have hidden us. A giant animal with antlers that looked a lot like a deer except super-sized ran by at top speed, knocking limbs and leaves from trees. It was so heavy that its footprints left huge holes in the ground. Nobody said a word until it was well out of sight.

"Daniel, what was that?" I asked. "Because it sure looked like one of the monsters to me."

Daniel crossed his arms and tried to not look scared to death. "Fine. Most of the monsters are outside the gate. But I guess they contained a few of them."

"That was the Ceryneian Hind!" Mia said. "It's just one more reason why this is a really bad idea."

I pulled my spear off my back and held it in my free hand. I could throw it one-handed if I had to, and since I still had my shield and wasn't going to let go of the apple, that was the best I could do.

"Come one, you guys," I said. "Let's spend the night back at the bunk."

We wound our way through camp until we got to the Team Hydra bunk. The Camp Hercules flag still hung out front, waving in the wind, though there were a few holes in it, maybe from where Amazon arrows had gone through it. But aside from the sound of the flag flapping, there wasn't another sound.

"Where do you think everyone is?" Daniel said.

"Guarding the gate," Harper said. "They have to be."

After the monsters had attacked, our bunk had been the only one still standing, so if any of the counselors were sleeping, it would have been here.

"Or maybe they're all gone," Mia said. "Because, like I said, this is a really bad idea."

I didn't understand why she thought this was such a bad

idea, but the more she mentioned it, the less I wanted to talk to her. Still, she was Harper's roommate, so I flashed her a quick smile and then hurried inside the bunk.

The first thing I did was check out the pantry. Score! It was stocked with food. Not good food, but any food was good right now as far as I was concerned. I was starving. We all ate, then went to bed.

The next morning, we grabbed a quick breakfast from the pantry, then set out, toward Mount Olympus.

"So what is this Sphinx thing that Prometheus mentioned?" I asked. I'd held off for as long as I could, since I was sure it was horrible.

Mythology did not disappoint.

"It's a monster with the head of a woman, the body of a lion, the wings of an eagle, and a snake for a tail," Mia said. "If you can't solve her riddle, she'll eat you. You should never go near the Sphinx. Everyone knows that."

"Oh, but we have to," Daniel said. "You see when we—"

"We just have to," I said, cutting him off. I didn't want to tell Mia about the promise that we'd made Prometheus.

"Well, I don't think it's a good idea," Mia said. "And I'm sure Zeus and Hera wouldn't think so either. I'd tell you to ask Zeus, you now, since he's supposedly your grandfather and all, but whatever."

She said this last part like she didn't actually believe Zeus would be related to me.

"What do you mean, supposedly?" I said. "My mom told me he was my grandfather. It's not like my mom would lie about something like that."

Mia put her hands on her hips. "Who's your grand-mother?"

It was a really good question. Mom had always said her mother was dead, and I'd had no reason to question that. But with this whole related-to-the-gods thing, it certainly made the question more important.

I shook my head. "It doesn't matter."

We started toward Mount Olympus, heading toward base camp. The more we walked, the stranger it was that no one was around. I was about to open my mouth and ask why, when there was a giant explosion.

"It's our bunk!" Daniel shouted, pointing where we'd just come from.

Sure enough, behind us was the remains of the Team Hydra bunk, engulfed in flames. Flaming arrows shot through the air. One hit the flag and it burst into flames. Then one of the arrows came right for us.

"Run!" Harper shouted, and we took off as fast as we could. There was no going back the way we'd come.

# CHAPTER 46

We left the explosion behind and dashed toward base camp. The black charred remains of Lucky Rock were still there, but that was about the only thing recognizable. The flag pole had been knocked over. The nearby dining hall was in ruins. And the ground was torn up from animal hooves.

"Camp is destroyed," Harper said.

"Yeah," I said, hurrying for the base of Mount Olympus. Last time the mountain had given us protection.

"What are they going to do about it?" Harper said. She almost looked like she was going to cry.

"Who cares?" Mia said. "This whole camp was a bad idea from the very start."

I had no clue what to say in response. The closer we got to our destination, the sourer Mia's attitude got. I really wished we could have left her back outside the walls of Camp Hercules because all she was doing at this point was bringing us down.

"I care," I said. It was really funny. A couple weeks ago, I would have been thrilled if camp had been called off from the very start. But now? I was totally invested. I not only wanted this curse broken, but once it was, I was willing to help rebuild camp if I had to. I wanted to spend the rest of summer here. And the summer after that.

"Yeah, well . . . ," Mia said. But she didn't say anything else because Harper scowled at her.

We started up Mount Olympus, and even though we'd been this way a few times before, nothing looked the same. We climbed to where I was sure Prometheus had been chained to the rocks, but there was no sign of the chains or Itchy and Scratchy, the eagles who'd been tormenting him for years.

When we got to the halfway point, we finally saw something familiar.

"It's Hercules' house," Harper said.

"Is he home?" Daniel didn't wait before running up to the front door of the place. There was no sign of the harpy who had attacked us when we stole the amphora, and there was no sign of Hercules.

I peeked in a window. "I don't think anyone is here."

Camp was deserted.

"They're all at the wall," Harper said. "We need to keep going."

We got back on the path and took one step toward the top of Mount Olympus when thunder rumbled in the sky.

Everyone stopped and looked at me.

"What?" I said.

"Do we keep going?" Daniel said.

I clutched the apple in my fist. We had to get it to the top.

"Yeah, we keep going." I didn't know why he was asking me. I wasn't the leader or anything. But neither was anyone else, so I guess I was going to have to do.

Thunder rumbled again, but this time we kept going, climbing higher and higher. All I could see were clouds covering the top of the mountain. But whatever was up there, we were going to have to face it. I just didn't realize it would be so soon.

Out of the clouds dipped three flying monsters.

"Harpies!" Daniel screamed. "Find cover!"

# CHAPTER 47

The harpies flew at us, one after another. They were green and had claws that could have wrapped around my stomach and snapped me in half. And their teeth were at least four times bigger than they needed to be. But that wasn't the worst of it. The worst part was the shrieking noise they let out every time they made a nosedive for us.

We dashed under some rocks that hung out over the side of the mountain. That was great for the moment, but we need to get past them.

"We need something shiny," I said, looking right at Daniel.

"What?" he said. "I already gave you my lucky quarter. I don't have another."

Next I looked to Harper and then Mia who both shook their heads.

"What about the apple?" Mia said, reaching for it like she was going to grab it out of my hand.

"No way!" I said. "We can't give them the apple." Sure it was shiny, but it was the entire reason we were here.

"But if we don't, they'll kill us," Mia said.

I shook my head. "Not if we fight them off." I wasn't sure what bravery had gotten into me, but I tucked the apple into my pocket. It was big and bulky, but I needed both hands. Before anyone could say another word, I grabbed my sword and shield, and then shoved the golden crown onto my head.

Daniel gasped even though he'd seen it before. Harper smiled. And Mia scowled.

Whatever.

I jumped from behind the rocks and ran out toward the harpies, swinging my sword like a crazy person. But I also tried to remember everything that Atty and Jason had taught us in weapons training. These were real monsters that would kill me if I wasn't careful.

Maybe they couldn't see me, but they could smell me. One let out a horrible shriek and dove right where I was standing. I rolled out of the way just in time, and then swiped out at it with my sword.

It was a perfect hit. The harpy evaporated into a giant puff of smoke as the sword sliced through it.

One down. Two to go.

The other two harpies weren't too happy that I'd destroyed their trio. They both dove at me at once. I still had the advantage that they couldn't see me. This time I rolled forward, passing right under them. Their claws brushed my camp T-shirt, but didn't cut through. I was never so happy for the thing. Then, I turned around and swiped my sword through the air again, connecting with one of the harpies. It turned into a giant cloud of dust like the first had.

Two down. One to go. The final one was so mad, she lashed out over and over again, raking her claws through the rocks, digging near my toes. I backed up and up and up.

"Watch out, Logan!" Harper shouted.

They couldn't see me, but I guess they could see what was happening. I dared to glance behind me. I was at the edge of a cliff. One more step and I would go over. I only had one option.

I grabbed hold of the harpy's giant claw before it could grab me, and hung on. It flew up into the air, shaking its leg like it was trying to get rid of me. But I had the better position. I waited until it was above solid ground, and then I swiped with the sword one more time.

The harpy exploded into dust. And since I no longer had anything to hold onto, I fell to the ground hard. The crown got knocked from my head and rolled a few feet away.

"Nice job!" Harper said. She ran over and gave me a high five.

"Is that all of them?" I asked. I was going to be in real trouble if there were three more hiding in the shadows.

"That's it," Daniel said. "All the myths say that they travel in packs of three."

"Great." I stood and reached for the crown, but Mia stooped down and picked it up before I could get to it.

"This is pretty cool," she said.

I held my hand out. "Yeah, and it's mine, so can you give it back?"

She immediately handed it over. But there was something about the way she looked at it, like she didn't want to give it back.

"No problem," Mia said. "You know it's not too late to turn around."

I didn't bother responding. Instead I tucked away my sword and the crown, made sure the apple was still secure, and then started back up Mount Olympus.

"The cave should be inside the cloud line," Daniel said, catching up to me.

Harper hurried up to us also. "What about the riddle?"

"No one can solve the riddle," Mia said.

"I don't know," Daniel said. "I'm pretty good at riddles."

I really hoped he was right.

"Why are we stopping here again?" Mia asked.

I thought fast. I needed to tell her something so she'd stop asking about it.

"It's a dare," I said. "Some kid from Team Apple dared us to do it."

"A dare?" Mia looked like she didn't believe a word I was saying, but the dare thing was the best thing I could come up with.

"Yep, a dare," Harper said, backing me up. "Can't back down from a dare."

"That's stupid," Mia said.

"Stupid or not, a dare is a dare," I said.

When we passed through the line of clouds, a few things happened. First, it got a lot cooler, making me wish we'd gotten Camp Hercules jackets also. Second, it got really quiet. So quiet that when something shrieked out, I jumped. I had no idea what it was, but I was willing to bet that whatever it was, we didn't want to run into it. And third, everything green disappeared. Below the clouds, the mountain had trees and grass and bushes, but up here, it was all rocks. I still couldn't see a palace at the top of the mountain, but with everything else, I was sure it was up there.

"Guys," Harper said. She stopped walking.

"What?"

"I think the cave is over that way." She motioned to the right, to a huge bunch of rocks, most bigger than Prometheus.

"How do you know?" I asked. There were rocks everywhere.

She tapped her foot on the ground. "There's a trail."

Once I looked, I wished I hadn't. The ground was covered in bones, and Harper was right. They made a perfect trail off to the right, directly toward the rocks.

"Oh," Daniel said, and every bit of color drained from his face.

I clapped him on the shoulder. "Remember, you're good at riddles. She won't eat you."

Daniel gulped. "Yeah, you're right." Then he straightened his fanny pack and bandana and set off, down the trail of bones.

They crunched under his feet as he walked, and since that was the only noise around, it sounded extra awful. I was probably going to have nightmares about it, if we survived this whole Sphinx thing.

Daniel stopped at a giant rock at the end of the trail. Then he pressed his body against it and leaned around, like he was trying to get a better look.

Something jumped out into the path. And sure, Mia had described the Sphinx, but seeing it here, in real life, was way worse. It wasn't so much the appearance—body of a lion, eagle's wings, and a tail that was actually a hissing snake. It was the calm look on the face. So calm, almost like the Sphinx was counting the seconds before she would be able to eat us and add our bones to the piles lining the trail. To make matters worse, she licked her lips.

# CHAPTER 48

"Hello, brave travelers," the Sphinx said. "It shall be noted upon your deaths that you dared to approach the cave rather than cowering back at the foot of the trail."

Well, that was just perfect. At least if anyone ever heard about our failure, they'd think we were brave. Or stupid. Yeah, stupid was definitely more like it, because seriously, what had we been thinking coming here? Mia was right (which I couldn't believe I was saying). We should have skipped this little detour and walked right up to the door of the gods' palace and knocked.

Except we needed to bring Prometheus the key.

But maybe Daniel wasn't having the same doubts as me because he stepped forward and put his hands on his hips.

"What's your riddle?" he asked.

The Sphinx laughed, but then she started coughing like she had a bone caught in her throat

"Right, the riddle," she managed to say. "Yes, we do have to get the formalities out of the way before I eat you."

"You won't eat us," Daniel said. "I'll solve your riddle, then you'll give us the key and let us continue on our way."

The Sphinx laughed again. "Whatever you say, brave camper. Okay, the riddle."

"Wait!" Daniel said. "Don't make it the one about the four legs then two legs then three legs. Everyone knows the answer to that."

I had no clue what he was talking about. I looked to Harper who shrugged and shook her head.

"You're sure?" the Sphinx said. "Okay, I'll go with a different one then."

Daniel was an idiot, even if he was really smart. Did he seriously just give up the chance to answer a riddle he knew the answer to? If he didn't get eaten, I might shave his head, for revenge.

"Hit me up!" Daniel said.

The Sphinx did the coughing laugh again, then cleared her throat and spit out a giant loogie. It was totally gross, but I wasn't going to say anything about it.

"What has one head, one foot, and four legs?" the Sphinx asked, then bared her teeth.

Daniel didn't even hesitate.

"A bed."

The mouth of the Sphinx dropped open. "You knew it?"

"No, I didn't know it," Daniel said. "But it's kind of easy.

You should consider some harder riddles. You know I could come by sometime, after this whole adventure is over, and we could go over some. I have some really great riddles I've learned."

The Sphinx's face broke into a huge smile. Then she licked her lips again, but this time, it wasn't so much that she wanted to eat us, but maybe more like the air was actually pretty dry up here.

"That would be acceptable," the Sphinx said.

Great. Daniel was making plans to have tea with a monster from Greek mythology.

The Sphinx disappeared behind the rock and hopefully into her cave. When she came back out, she held a giant golden key in her teeth. She leaned forward and presented it to Daniel who took it and tucked it into his fanny pack.

"Maybe next week," the Sphinx said.

"Sounds great!" Daniel turned back to us and grinned. I could not believe that not only had he gotten the key, he'd made a monster friend. Camp Hercules had to be the craziest place in the entire world.

The Sphinx went back into her cave and didn't come out, so we set off, down the trail of bones. We walked for a good half hour, so long that my legs started cramping. I was about to suggest we stop for a snack when something shiny caught my eye.

I glanced up and shielded my eyes because whatever it was, it was really bright. And once the sun glare vanished it came into view. Ahead of us was the most magnificent palace I'd ever seen in my entire life. It was pure gold and so tall that Prometheus could have walked in it without stooping. Giant steps also made of gold led up to the front of it, and the sun seemed to shine right on it, casting the bright gold everywhere.

We had reached the home of the gods.

# CHAPTER 49

The four of us stood there, looking up at the palace. I tried really hard to figure out something funny or snarky to say, but nothing would come out of my mouth. We had done it. We'd climbed to the top of Mount Olympus, avoided being killed, and found the home of the gods.

"So you grandfather lives here?" Harper said.

Weird butterflies ran through my stomach. I was having a really hard time imagining my grandpa, the guy who'd taken me to McDonald's on weekends, living here in this golden palace.

"Yeah, it's kind of strange."

All thoughts of having a snack vanished from my mind. There was only one thing that mattered now: completing our mission.

"Here's the plan," I said. "We sneak up there and surprise them. We can use the key to get inside. And hopefully since I'm related, the gods won't zap us with a lightning bolt or anything like that."

"Why do we have to sneak?" Mia said.

I turned to face her. "Because even though Zeus may be on my side, Hera is kind of mean."

Mia crossed her arms. "She's not mean."

"She put a curse on camp," Harper said. "That's pretty mean."

"She put the curse on Hercules," Mia said. "He's the one responsible for bringing it to camp. He's the one who should be here."

"But he's not," I said. "Which means we need to take care of this now."

We tiptoed up the path, hiding behind rocks on our way. Luck was on our side because nothing happened. No thunder or lightning or eagles or harpies. Everything was going perfectly.

We got to the tall staircase leading up to the front gate. I went first, even though Daniel still had the key. Whatever bravery he'd had back with the Sphinx had vanished. When we got to the top he scooted past me and put the key in the lock. The gate swung open without a sound. We were in.

Harper closed the gate behind us, and we took off down a white marble hallway with all sorts of gold accents. The entire place was really fancy, like someone had taken a can of gold paint and made sure there was a smattering of it at least every two feet.

We rounded a corner and I heard voices. Immediately I jumped behind a golden column that reached all the way up to the ceiling. I dared to peek around the side.

There was a giant amphora in the room, a lot like the one that had been broken at camp except probably three times as tall. Two people sat at a table playing chess. One I recognized immediately. It was my grandpa. He looked exactly the same as he'd always looked, with curly gray hair, a blue T-shirt, and blue jeans. The other person was a woman with dark hair piled really high on her head, making her at least a foot taller than she really was. She had a purple T-shirt and jeans on, and had peacock feathers sticking out of her massive hair. I guess it was casual Friday here on Mount Olympus.

"That's Hera," Daniel whispered from next to me.

But I guess his whisper was a little loud, because both of them immediately looked our way.

"Hey there, Logan," Grandpa said. "You're a long way from camp."

I stepped out from behind the column. There was no point in hiding now.

"Hey, Grandpa," I said. "You never told me you were a god." Might as well get right to it.

He scratched his head. "Would you have believed me?"

I shook my head. "Probably not. But still, it's kind of major."

Grandpa (or Zeus—I wasn't sure how to exactly think of him) stood up from the chess board and started toward me. "You mother and I wanted to wait until we thought you were ready to know."

"And you thought I was ready now?"

"No, but sometimes things don't work out exactly like we plan." He gave me a hug and ruffled my hair and the whole thing was really strange.

Harper, Daniel, and Mia stepped into view.

"I brought some friends with me," I said.

Zeus smiled. Hera, on the other hand, looked like she'd swallowed a lemon.

"I don't remember you four being granted permission to come here," she said.

"Well, there's a very good reason for that," Daniel stammered. He clenched his hands into fists like he was trying to channel bravery into himself.

Now was as good a time as any. I grabbed the apple from my pocket and pulled it out. "We brought you something."

Hera's mouth twisted up into a smile. "I'd love to say that this is a surprise, but then I'd be lying."

She raised an eyebrow, and before I knew what was happening, Mia ran to me and grabbed the apple. I tried to grab it back, but it was too late.

We'd been completely tricked. Mia was the spy of Hera who'd infiltrated our camp, and now she was going to ruin our perfect plan.

# CHAPTER 50

"No way!" Harper shouted. She grabbed the circle chakram thing from the hook at her waist and whipped it directly at Mia. Her aim was perfect. It hit the golden apple, knocking it from Mia's hand. The apple flew against the wall, and then rolled back, stopping right at Daniel's feet. He grabbed it and clenched it between both his hands.

Mia ran forward like she was going to try to get it back, but Harper grabbed the circle thing from the air as it zipped back to her, and then tackled Mia, pinning her to the ground. It was so epic that if I hadn't seen it with my own eyes, I never would have believed it.

"You're the spy!" Harper shouted. "I trusted you. You were my roommate, and here, you've been working against us this entire time."

"So what?" Mia said, twisting her head around. "I can't believe you guys would seriously think you could go up against Hera, queen of the gods. Do you have any idea who you're actually dealing with?"

I glanced over to Hera. She looked half proud, half annoyed that her spy had been caught. And thankfully Daniel still had the apple.

I stepped forward, trying to act really cool and calm even though my heart felt like it was going to pound right out of my chest. "We're here to make a deal."

Hera tipped her head back and laughed. "A deal. Please."

"The golden apple in exchange for breaking the curse," I said, trying to keep my confidence even though it felt like it was going to slip out the bottom of my feet and disappear where I would never find it again.

"Please," Hera said. "I would never make that deal."

Zeus cleared his throat. "I don't know, dear. I think you might want to listen."

Hera frowned. "That's nonsense. It doesn't matter if you have my spy. She's served her purpose, letting me know you were coming. I don't need her anymore."

"What?" Mia said. "You promised me you'd grant me three wishes."

Hera laughed. "Three wishes. What do I look like? A genie?"

"But you promised!" Mia cried.

I almost felt kind of sorry for Mia, but then I remembered that because of her, all the Labors of Hercules were out destroying the world. And we needed to stop them.

"Do we have a deal?" I said.

"Never," Hera said. She put her hand out, toward Daniel and the apple, like she expected it to fly into her hands.

Nothing happened.

Okay, that wasn't quite true. The sour look on her face grew, and she shoved her hand out again. And again. And still nothing happened.

Hera bit her lip and glanced to Zeus. He smiled.

"Is there a problem, dear?"

"Yes, there's a problem. They have my apple, and I want it back." Hera sounded like she was throwing a giant temper tantrum. I bet she would have stomped her foot if it wouldn't have been too un-goddesslike.

"Well," Zeus said. "If you want the apple, I can think of one way to get it."

Hera crossed her arms. "No. I won't do it."

"Then no apple," Daniel said. He started to put it into his fanny pack.

"I guess we'll be on our way then," I said. It was really weird, with my grandpa in the same room. Somehow I knew he was responsible for the apple not coming to Hera. I didn't know how, but it had to be him. I glanced at him, and he winked at me.

"Wait!" Hera said. Her eyes glistened as she stared at the apple. "What are the terms of your deal?"

I tried really hard to keep the smile from my face.

"The curse gets broken," I said. "Completely. And you can't start it up again. You have to stop the labors and bring them all back to camp where they can be kept safely inside the walls of Camp Hercules."

"Absolutely not!" Hera said.

Zeus cleared his throat. "It's been long enough. It's time to let your grudge against Hercules go. You're destroying the world. It's not very nice."

"But Hercules shows no respect," Hera said.

"So you don't want the apple?" I said. "I guess we'll be going then."

I turned, acting like I was going to leave. I figured we could leave Mia here and the gods could deal with her.

"Oh, fine," Hera said. "Those are your terms? And if I meet them, you'll give me the apple?"

I almost said yes, right then. But I didn't want camp to be over. I also didn't want to spend the rest of summer rebuilding Greek temples if I didn't have to.

"You also have to restore Camp Hercules to exactly how it was before," I said.

A huge smile broke out on Daniel's face. "Yeah, exactly. But add a taco stand near the river."

Hera twisted up her mouth into a frown. "Fine. I accept your terms. I'll break the curse and restore your camp if you give me the apple."

She held her hand out. But did she think we were stupid?

"Break the curse first," Harper said. She still gripped the circle thing at her waist.

Hera put a finger to her lips and glanced at the amphora. "I don't have anything to break it with."

That was it. The curse was inside the amphora, just like Hercules had contained the labors inside his amphora.

Everything would be better once they both were broken. We were halfway there.

Harper didn't hesitate. The circle thing zipped out again and struck the side of the giant amphora. A tiny little crack formed and the weapon returned to Harper's hand. Then the crack grew and the entire thing shattered, almost imploding into a giant pile of dust and rubble on the marble ground.

Daniel glanced at me, and I nodded. He walked forward, even though it looked like every part of his body was shaking, and placed the apple in Hera's outstretched hand.

There was a weird awkward silence, and I tried to think of something witty to say. But luckily I was saved because right then Mom and Athena walked into the room.

Mom held a live peacock in her hands.

"Are we late?" Athena asked, looking around at the situation. I guess she figured out that we'd done it—we'd broken the curse—because she looked at me and smiled.

"Late for what?" Hera said with a small smile. She held the apple, and it seemed to have some sort of calming effect on her.

"We brought you a gift," Mom said, walking forward with the peacock. She set it at Hera's feet and stepped back.

"A gift?" Hera said. "And what do you want in exchange for it?"

Mom stopped when she got next to me. "Nothing, of course. It's just a gift."

They'd brought the peacock to make the same deal that we had. But we'd gotten here first. I grinned, but Mom leaned over and whispered, "Don't get too happy. You're seriously grounded after this."

"But—" I started. She couldn't be serious. We'd saved the world.

"We'll talk about this later," Mom said.

I wasn't sure who was scarier: Hera, queen of the gods, or Mom when she was angry.

Zeus walked over and hugged Mom, and I finally felt like he was just my grandpa again. And since we were all there and it would have been rude otherwise, we stayed for lunch. Even Mia. Of course she sat at the end of the table and refused to talk to anyone, but I couldn't do anything about that. I kind of felt like there should be some bigger punishment for her. I mean, if I was going to be grounded for saving the world, then she should at least have to clean up cow poop for the rest of the summer. But that wasn't really my problem. As far as I knew, my problems were all over.

# CHAPTER 51

If I thought anything was going to change, you know, since I was the grandson of a god, I was completely wrong. No sooner was lunch over, Mom turned to me.

"Time to go back to camp," she said. "And if I hear anything about you messing around or breaking the rules, you'll be grounded for life."

"I'd never break the rules," I said.

Mom only looked at me. I would have sworn that Zeus covered his mouth to keep from laughing, but I didn't say anything about it.

"Never come up here again," Hera said, and then without another word, she left the room.

"Sorry about that," Zeus said. "Come visit anytime you want." Then he hugged me again and left the room following after Hera.

Athena also cut out right after that, taking Mia with her. Mia looked half-flattered to be in the company of her favorite goddess and half terrified, like she was sure she was going to get turned into a toad. I hoped she did.

That left Mom to walk down the side of Mount Olympus with us. It took way less time going down, almost like she knew some kind of short cut.

When we got to the bottom, Daniel rushed over to the center of base camp.

"No way! It's Lucky Rock."

I looked over. Sure enough, there was Lucky Rock, in its perfect golden condition, like it had never been struck by lightning. And off to the side was the flagpole, with the Camp Hercules flag flying proudly at the top. The dining hall had been rebuilt completely, as had every other single gazebo and fire pit. Even the grass was perfect, as if hundreds of wild animal monsters hadn't trampled all over it.

"I can't believe she got it done this quickly," Harper said.

Mom gave us a small smile. "Never underestimate the power of the gods."

Just then Hercules sauntered up to us, followed by Jason and Atty and most of the other counselors.

"I'm pleased to say that the curse had been broken," Hercules said. He stood all tall, like somehow he was completely responsible for breaking the curse himself.

I was about to open my mouth and tell him everything that had gone on, but Mom raised an eyebrow, as if to say, 'Are you sure you want to do that?'

Come to think of it, I wasn't sure. Maybe, if the gods had

their secrets, it was okay for us to have our own secrets, too.

"That's awesome!" I said, casting a glance at Harper and Daniel. They caught on perfectly.

"Way to go!" Harper said.

"You're the best!" Daniel said.

Hercules stood taller with each compliment.

Mom left, and slowly the other campers started filing in. Some of the counselors had been sent out to find them. Once everyone was there, we had the most epic campfire in all of history, with so many s'mores that my stomach hurt after eating them.

We started walking back to the bunk, but Jason caught up to us quickly.

"I'm guessing there's more to the story," Jason said.

I laughed before I could stop myself. "Yeah, just a little. Nothing big."

Jason waited.

"Fine," I said. "There may have been a grouchy old sea god, a dragon with one hundred heads, three vampire nymphs, some harpies, and the Sphinx, but that's about it."

Jason laughed. "That's it? You're sure?"

"Oh, and a golden apple," I said. "But nothing else."

"Good job," Jason said. "You kids did great. And Logan, in the morning, go by the Trading Post and get yourself a new bandana."

I gulped. The Trading Post. I'd have to see the Fates at the Trading Post, and then I'd have to settle the whole capturing Prometheus thing. It almost took away the great feeling the campfire had given me. Almost.

"Sure thing," I said.

Without another word, Jason walked off.

"What about the key?" Harper said. "We still have to give it to Prometheus."

"Yeah, do you really think that's a good idea?" Daniel said. "You know, especially since Zeus is your grandpa and all that. He might be mad."

Not only mad. Giving the Titan the key to Mount Olympus could also put Zeus in danger. And I wasn't sure I could do that. Actually I was sure that I couldn't do that. I just had to figure out a way to get out of it. But tomorrow was a great day to figure that out. For now, I planned to enjoy the rest of my evening as one of the epic heroes who saved Camp Hercules.

# THE END

# TWELVE
# LABORS/BUNKS
# OF HERCULES

**1. Team Lion:**

Slay the Nemean lion

**2. Team Hydra:**

Slay the nine-headed
Lernaean Hydra

**3. Team Hind:**

Capture the Ceryneian Hind

**4. Team Boar:**

Capture the Erymanthian Boar

**5. Team Cow Stable:**

Clean the Augean stables in a single day

**6. Team Bird:**

Slay the Stymphalian birds

**7. Team Cretan Bull:**

Capture the Cretan Bull

**8. Team Horse:**

Steal the Horses of
Diomedes

**9. Team Belt:**

Obtain the Belt of Hippolyta, Queen of
the Amazons

**10. Team Cattle:**

Obtain the Cattle of the monster Geryon

**11. Team Apple:**

Steal the apples of the Hesperides

**12. Team Cerberus:**

Capture and bring back Cerberus

# RULES OF CAMP HERCULES

**Camp Rule Number One:**

Every morning, every camper touches Lucky Rock.

**Camp Rule Number Two:**

No one ever touches the amphora.

**Camp Rule Number Three:**

Wear your T-shirt and bandana at all times.

**Camp Rule Number Four:**

Carry your sword with you at all times.

**Camp Rule Number Five:**

Carry your spear with you at all times.

**Camp Rule Number Six:**

Don't break curfew.

## ABOUT THE AUTHOR

If P. J. Hoover had to pick one of the Labors
of Hercules, it would definitely be Team Apple
because a golden apple would look great on P. J.'s
bookshelf. Also, the apples probably taste amazing.
P. J. lives in Austin, Texas and dreams up ways to
sneak mythology into every single book written.

To contact P. J. Hoover:

pjhoover@pjhoover.com

www.pjhoover.com

47394624R00179

Made in the USA
Middletown, DE
06 June 2019